PROLOGUE

Year 1308 BCE

M edusa

The rage of the gods was clear.

The waves gnashed at the shore, sea foam spewing over the weathered rocks as the storm rolled in. I stood on the beach as the clouds gathered, wondering what had angered the great gods. There was a sickly green tint to the sky, interrupted by the occasional jagged strike of lightning in the distance.

Electric tension charged the air. It clung to me like a second skin, making the serpents around my head writhe with displeasure.

A snap of lightning struck the beach close by, making me

hiss. I averted my gaze from the blinding light, my scales vibrating with the ferocity of it.

It was time to retreat to my cave, away from the eyes of the Fates. I'd been on this island for years now, and I preferred the solitude. The storm would roll through, another day of living without *men* to tell me what to do.

I moved quickly, my tail dragging across the sand. My wings pulled in close to my back, the feathers damp as the rain fell harder.

I came to the mouth of my cave, ready to dive into the icy darkness, but a noise made me freeze.

A shout.

"Help!"

I turned slowly, raising my brows as a figure fought their small boat.

"What kind of fool would be out on the water?"

I simply stared as a wave came upon them, capsizing the vessel. Once they drowned, I would return to my cave.

My stomach twisted as a head came back above the water, fighting hard. I snorted. They didn't stand a chance. The currents were too strong for a mortal.

That's why I chose this island. No one would interrupt my peace here.

And yet, here I was, watching someone drown. It was incredibly rude that they had done this right now. I had many things to do, of course. Like...

Well, I had nothing to do. But it was still rude of them.

They had yet to die.

I sighed, crossing my arms as I stared.

"Help!" they shouted again. *"Zeus! Bless me!"*

That made me smirk. As if a god would help them. The gods helped no one but themselves. That much had always been

Queens and Monsters

Three Fates Mafia Series
Book Three

Clio Evans

To all the girls who felt unlovable, who were told they were never enough, who felt like a monster hiding from society—I hope this book helps you rewrite your story because you are enough exactly as you are.

MORTALS BEWARE

Mortals Beware:

In this story, you will find the following:

Fisting, intense degradation, shibari, humiliation, BDSM, Dom/sub dynamics, murder, torture, graphic violence, mentions of assault, mentions of sexual assault, mentions of war and death, blackmail, flogging, spanking, sex toys, stabbing, electricity play, face sitting, breath play, Consensual Non Consent, chasing/primal hunting, and more.

If you have any questions, you can reach me on Instagram or Facebook, or via email clioevansauthor@gmail.com

clear. I was a monster, one of their many forgotten beings of creation.

I moved closer down the beach and glanced at the sky, scowling as the clouds parted. Surely the gods were not listening to this rat.

My scales slid over the sand as I came closer.

"Zeus, please! Father!"

They wore bronze armor, which would surely weigh them down.

They bobbed above the waves before being dragged back under. They were gone for one second...two...three...

But then they appeared again, sputtering water.

"Oh, for Hades' sake." I raised my hands to the sky. "Just take their soul, god of death, or have you lost your will?!"

Perhaps challenging the gods was a bad idea. I huffed, baring my fangs as I looked back out onto the crashing waves. The clouds continued to part, a single ray of sunshine falling on the drowning warrior, a beacon.

Was that a sign? A demand that I rescue them? I would do no such thing.

A wave swallowed them again, dragging them down into the briny depths. I let out a breath as the storm quieted, spreading my wings behind me and shaking them free of rain.

How peculiar this was.

I stayed for a few more minutes and then decided that Hades had claimed their lost soul.

My gaze stayed on the sea as the last brutal wave surged forth, rushing towards the shore. I moved back as it crashed against the sand, the pearly froth forming in long bands.

"Curses," I whispered.

A body washed up with that wave.

"Really?"

I stared at the dark figure on the sand. They laid there

unmoving for a few moments, and then lifted their head, throwing up seawater. They gagged and made a noise, somewhere between a groan and a choking sound.

Rage overcame me. I rushed to them, noting that they had lost all their armor aside from their helm. Now they would perish at my gaze, another statue to add to my collection. I grabbed them by their tunic and turned them over with a hiss, all the serpents around me lifting as I felt the power surge through me.

I met a piercing blue gaze.

They did not turn to stone. *Why* weren't they turning to stone?

I drew back as if they had struck me. "What kind of mortal man are you?" I snarled.

"I'm neither mortal nor man," they responded.

I stared as they reached up and pulled off their helm, throwing it to the side. Long brown hair unfurled, a strip of silver at the front. They had dark brows and sun kissed skin. My gaze roamed their body again. Their chiton had pushed up their slender thighs, almost too high.

Indeed, they were not a man. But they should have turned to stone. Instead, they looked at me the same way I looked at them.

"Who are you?" I asked, alarmed. "If you are not mortal, then *what* are you?"

"I am Perseus, Daughter of Zeus," she said.

A low laugh left me. A demigod. A daughter, no less. A *woman*. All the demigods I'd ever known were men.

"You must be a disappointment," I said, leaning back.

"I am not." Her face flushed, her eyes reminding me of the storm. "Did you not see how the gods aided me? They know I am a great hero."

I stared at her for a moment, torn between amusement and

anger. I hated demigods. If she was here on purpose, that meant they had sent her to kill me.

"I saw nothing but a poor seaman, *woman*, who would have drowned had not the wave drawn you to shore," I said, rising. "From the sea you came, to the sea you shall return. Swim back home, little girl. This island is full of scary monsters."

I turned, heading back for my cave. I wanted to roast some fish over a fire. I could enjoy the setting sun now that the storm had suddenly rolled away—

"Wait!" she called. "Wait! I need your help!"

My *help*?!

I spun on her as she got to her feet, running after me. Her chiton fell to her mid thighs, her sandaled feet sinking into the sand. She grabbed her helm and ran after me.

"Can you not see I am a *monster*?" I hissed as she stopped in front of me.

She gave me a soft smile, her blue gaze lifting to my snakes and then to my lower half, and then to my breasts.

I'd been living alone for so long, I'd forgotten that I should probably cover them. Heat flooded me, my nipples perking up. I maintained my deadly glare, wishing Hades had finished the job instead of being a coward. The Fates were fickle.

"I can. But you are one of great beauty. Unlike some others I've fought. They sent me here to behead you, but I don't want to. I think we can work together."

"No," I said immediately. "If you follow me, then I will send you to the underworld."

"Come on," she pleaded. "What can I do to show you I'm trying to help you by not killing you?"

"I don't need nor want your help, peasant," I snarled. "As if you could kill me."

"Listen," she said, "I am only here because a king is to wed my mother. He is awful. There is only one way I can save her.

He demanded that I bring him your head for her freedom. I believe I can fool him."

"Of course you can," I said. "He's a man. But you don't need my help for that."

"I do," she said. "I really do."

Despite all of my instincts screaming for me to kill her, I turned, moving back towards my cave. There was something about her.

Perhaps it was me that was the fool.

I paused, glancing over my shoulder at her. "Well? Come on, you stupid girl."

"I'm a woman," she argued, but she smiled and followed.

Girl, woman, demigod. I would simply kill her in her sleep.

Chapter 1

Virgin Mimosas

P ercy

I sat across from Madeline at the table, both of us sandwiched between angry, brooding men.

Well—angry, brooding demigods and monsters.

I drummed my fingertips on the cold oak top as I listened to Orpheus and Damon argue. The two of them were going in circles once again over the missing knife. We all believed someone had stolen it, but no one was certain who the thief was.

Damon was the leader of the Cerberus branch, run with Minos and Aaecus. The three of them made up the massive monster. Orpheus was the leader of his own branch, a demigod that was just as bad as the two that had died recently.

Hercules and Jason.

I couldn't say I missed either one of them. For years, I'd been the only female demigod at the table. It was a nice change when Serena and Ashley were present.

"Someone has stolen the knife," Orpheus snarled, slamming his fist down. The table rattled. "The knife that belonged to *me*. A gift from my father! From a god!"

Ian growled, leaning forward in his seat next to Damon. "You know, you don't need to remind us that your father is a god every time we fucking meet, Orpheus. Nothing has changed in the last few centuries."

Orpheus sneered. "Just reminding you of your place, *monster*."

I rolled my eyes.

The Three Fates Mafia didn't run itself. And the leaders were a ragtag group of rejects that the Fates had forced together into one city, made to share our broken toys. It had never been my favorite solution, but it kept both sides from destroying one another.

Things were slowly changing. Over the last couple years, monsters and demigods had come together, shaking up my belief that we could never be. The three men that made up Cerberus were mated to the demigod Ashley. Ian, the Colchian Dragon, was mated to the demigod Serena, and their human partner.

It was the dawn of a new era.

My gaze slid to Madeline's. Even behind her sunglasses, I could feel the mischief and amusement there. Both of us had become accustomed to letting the men go round and round until we got bored.

The ceiling fan creaked. It smelled like sweat. I glanced down the table, wishing that Serena and Ashley were here, but they'd entrusted their monstrous husbands to vouch for them, which left me with an old, crusty, Theseus and an even older Orpheus.

Theseus looked like he was half asleep, his eyes narrow slits as he listened to Orpheus bellow.

It felt like old times without the newer demigods here, and not in a good way. Cerberus and the Colchian Dragon were unbalanced without their mates, and their fury was bleeding into the room.

The shouting match began. I sighed, leaning back in my seat. I tuned them out.

Orpheus' sacred knife was missing, the same one that Jason had driven into my leg. On stormy days like today, it still ached. It was hard to tell if it was genuine pain or just my mind focusing on the blade. I guessed that was part of getting older— but for an immortal demigod like me; it was strange. Maybe because it was a cursed blade, and I'd been lucky I was a demigod, or maybe because I was losing my touch... Either way, I rubbed my thigh absentmindedly, soothing myself.

The blade was a valuable piece. I was curious about who could have stolen it, but it wasn't my problem. The blade meant nothing to me.

Orpheus claimed Ashley had stolen it, given that prior to being a mafia boss, she was a thief. That, of course, did not go over well with Cerberus.

I doubted Ashley or even Serena had anything to do with the missing knife. We all had enemies outside of our circle. Enemies that would do anything to bring us down. The Three Fates Mafia had given certain monsters a second chance to serve the Fates, but not all. There were other creatures in our world that sought vengeance.

Of course, I would not bring that up right now. Not while everyone was shouting like cavemen.

Madeline took a drag from her cigarette, blowing it out in a silver cloud towards me.

"Put that away," I hissed, waving my hand in the air.

She let out a feminine chuckle. She'd worn crimson lipstick today, a deep red that matched her dress. Her neckline was a deep v, her breasts pressing together as she leaned forward. "It's just smoke, Perseus."

"Yes, and it's a small room," I quipped, annoyed. "You know I hate smoke."

Damon and Orpheus were still going at it.

Madeline tilted her head, looking at them like they were ants. "How long should we let them continue?"

Ian was red in the face now, his iridescent eyes blazing. Damon looked like he was about to explode, Aaecus and Minos on edge, too.

If I had a dollar for every time I'd listened to them go on like this, I wouldn't need to collect checks from the Fates. Not that I really needed to anyway, but I wouldn't say no to the funds they sent all of us quarterly.

Part of me wondered if it was blood money, the other part of me wondered if it was simply apology money. Regardless, I was sick of listening to everyone bitch about the stolen blade.

I rolled my eyes and stood, my chair scraping over the floor, interrupting them. All eyes turned to me.

"This has been *something*," I said. "And fruitless without Serena and Ashley here."

"Serena has entrusted me to speak for her in her absence," Ian snarled. "She's my wife and—"

"I don't care," I cut him off. "Where are they, anyway?"

Silence. Cold gazes. There had never been a genuine friendship between me and the other side, and I could feel that now. Their wives were the only demigods they'd ever deemed respectable.

"When they decide to join, we will reconvene," I said. "Orpheus and Damon have been arguing for an hour. Nothing has come of this. If you want to bicker, do it on your own dime. I have a business to run and prefer not to listen to the constant droning of man-children."

I adjusted my tweed jacket and shoved my chair back, heading toward the door. Madeline rose too, putting out her cigarette on the table.

"I think perhaps we should consider that we aren't the only ones who...well, hate us," Madeline said casually. Of course, she'd come to the same conclusion. "Perhaps we should consider that someone else has taken the blade. Orpheus, honey, why don't you make us a little list of everyone who hates you? We'll review it next time we meet."

He looked like he was about to explode. I'd never seen his face turn so red.

It took every ounce of control not to laugh.

"Until next time, ladies," she said, blowing the last of the smoke at Orpheus.

"We're not done!" Damon barked, the veins bulging in his forehead.

I ignored him, heading towards the door. "I am, puppy boy."

That didn't go over well, but I didn't care. I left before he could shout, leaving the room swiftly.

Where the fuck were Ashley and Serena? They couldn't just skip meetings like this. I hadn't realized how much I relied on them to be the voice of reason. Even Luca, Ian and Serena's partner, wasn't around.

I strode down the cold hall, meeting two of my men. Diego and Eric. Their expressions were a mixture of amused and withdrawn, which meant they'd heard everything. Diego opened the door for me.

"We'll get the car, Mistress," he said.

"Thank you," I answered.

He left, Eric taking his place by my side. He wore a black suit, a gun gleaming at his hip. There were other men around too, guards that belonged to the other leaders. I could feel their eyes on us. No one trusted each other here.

I dragged in a breath of fresh air, my gaze raising to the sky.

Dark clouds were gathering in the distance. I'd always enjoyed storms. Maybe because I could feel the last remnants of power from our forgotten gods. But now, it came with the throb of pain, and with the reminder that I'd murdered another demigod.

"That was quite the show."

I turned, seeing Madeline step up next to me. Her scent hit me—vanilla and whisky and lust. I couldn't help but swallow hard.

"Your man can leave us," she said, nodding to him.

"Eric, give us a moment."

"Yes, Mistress." He left, stepping out of earshot.

"Such a good boy," Madeline purred. "You train them so well. Do you treat them how you treated the French army during the revolution?"

I snorted, glancing at her before looking back at the sky. "Which one, Madeline? There have been many revolutions."

I didn't have to look at her to know that she was smirking.

"Since when did you start smoking?" I asked. "That's a new habit."

"Well, I stopped drinking, like you told me."

"Well, stop smoking too," I said. "It's bad for your lungs."

"Are you worried about me?" she purred. She drew out a silver lighter, one that looked like lipstick, and struck a flame—lighting another cigarette.

"No," I said, stealing another glance at her. "Of course not. I don't worry about monsters."

We both smiled.

"Right," she said. "Well. Can you please retrieve the other girls for the next meeting? I can't say I've missed being thrown into a sausage fest."

"They're not children, Mads. They're grown women. And one of them is very pregnant so—"

"If they will not be mafia leaders, then they should just say so. I do not care about the reason. Unless one of them is actually birthing their monstrous spawn, they should be at these meetings."

I fought the urge to roll my eyes. Diego pulled our car up, parking it in front of me.

"You know, monsters and demigods can be together now," I mumbled.

It was no longer a crime as it had been for so long.

"Yes. Isn't that horrifying? Positively dreadful."

"Yes. Terrible," I echoed.

"Are you coming to my art show on Friday?" she asked.

"I bought tickets months ago," I said. "They always sell out so fast."

"Of course they do. Everyone wants to see my erotic statues. There was a man recently that made the mistake of disobeying me, and his equipment was rather large."

"I have no interest in men," I said.

"Oh, I'm aware," she mused. "I think you'll enjoy the other part of the exhibit. The women. I sculpted them with my hands instead of...well, you know."

Turning them to stone with her eyes. She could turn anyone to stone, but often used that ability on men. In fact, the only person who we knew of in the world who had yet to perish at her gaze was me.

Perhaps the entire world would think she was a villain if they knew that all the men they ogled in her exhibits were once living mortals. But I had no sympathy for them. They became stone because they didn't listen to her—or they were criminals that had done terrible things. She was merciless, but I had always appreciated that about her.

She showed me mercy.

"I know you're a boob gal. One of them has perfect tits. I mean, they're really stunning."

I chuckled. "I look forward to seeing them."

She nodded, and then let out a soft hum. "Are you worried about the missing knife? That blade is strong. In the wrong hands..."

"Not our problem," I said. "Whoever had the balls to steal from Ian is an idiot. And especially given that it belongs to Orpheus...I'm sure they'll take care of it. I'm certain it's someone outside the mafia, and in that case—they've attacked them. Not me. Not you."

It had nothing to do with us.

"True," she said.

"I'll see you Friday." I moved for the car door, but she beat me to it, opening it for me.

She lifted her sunglasses, her eyes meeting mine over the edge of the door. Golden irises with diamond pupils, the corners creasing as she smiled. It didn't matter that she was in her mortal form, her eyes never changed. They were the same as the day I'd washed up on her island centuries ago.

"Same time on Sunday?" she chimed. "Champagne for breakfast?"

"You just told me you stopped drinking," I hissed. "Hence the smoking now."

"Ugh. Fine. We'll have virgin mimosas, I suppose."

"I think that's just called orange juice," I mused.

She stared at me for a moment. "I think *virgin mimosas* sound better than orange juice, Percy. I heard they expanded the menu. Fresh croissants and fruit. You love croissants."

"Who doesn't love croissants?" I snorted. "They are perfect. One of the best things ever created."

"Someone like Orpheus who sucks the fun out of everything. I bet he doesn't like croissants," Madeline answered. "Or Argos. The Hydra men have no fun."

"Indeed. Well, I wouldn't miss it for the end of the world," I said. "I'll see you Friday, Mads."

She winked at me, putting her glasses back. I could feel everyone around us relax, no longer in danger of dying. I slid into the back seat. She shut the door, condemning me to solitude yet again.

"Where to, Mistress?" Diego asked.

I stared out the window for a moment, taking Madeline in. I never liked to say goodbye to her, even if I'd see her in a few days.

I'd never admit that to her, though. She'd make fun of me.

"Take me to my apartment on 5th Avenue," I said. "I'll be staying in the city until Sunday."

"For your date?"

My head whipped around and I narrowed my eyes on him. "Not a date, Diego. We're not even friends, just associates. It's a business lunch. Madeline despises demigods, remember?"

"Of course, Mistress," he said politely, but I could see the bastard smiling.

I sighed, looking out the window as raindrops pelted the glass. Madeline stood on the sidewalk as the others left the building. If I didn't know her or what she was, I might have worried seeing her surrounded by so many mafia men. Her crimson dress wavered as the wind became stronger, a headscarf wrapped around her dark brown hair rippling like a flag.

I liked the snakes more. And her wings and lower serpentine half. But I understood why she preferred to take her mortal form. Stolen from her so long ago, she now had it back because of the Fates. A gift from them.

She opened a compact mirror, reapplying her lipstick. Orpheus shot her a dark look as she forced him to go around her.

My gaze never left her as Diego pulled out onto the road, merging onto the highway that led back to Moirai.

THREE FATES MAFIA

PERCY

Chapter 2

Venom and Stone

M adeline

It was 6 P.M., and I was standing outside of the Moirai Art Museum. I should have been here at least 30 minutes ago, and the thought that I was late to my own show unnerved me.

It wasn't my fault the traffic had been so horrendous. But it was Friday, so perhaps I should have anticipated problems. If it wouldn't have ruined my dress, I would have simply changed into my monstrous form and gotten here faster. The only reason I would shred a dress this expensive is if it were out of passion.

I stared at the giant sign with my name on it. *Madeline Winters: An Erotic Masquerade Exhibition.*

"You're all set," Ella said, offering me a strained smile.

Ella was my new assistant, my little sidekick in crime. She had short bleached hair with bangs and wore a dress like mine, one that hid countless weapons.

She might have been new to my world, but she was doing

well. She kept my schedule together and took care of the things that annoyed me. I'd hired her after interviewing thirty different mortals, all who had irritated me. Hell, two of them had been so annoying I turned them to stone. They were even part of the exhibit tonight.

Then Ella had come along, I made her sign an NDA, and now here we were.

Ella was also clearly frazzled that we'd shown up late.

"Next time, we'll leave earlier," I said to her.

Ella nodded, placing my masquerade mask on my face. I stayed still as she tightened it around my head, adjusting my hair. "Of course. Is there anything else you need? One guard alerted me that the building is now at max capacity for the event. You sold out."

"Of course I sold out," I said. "People are thirsty for stone genitalia. I can't say much has changed since the days of Ancient Greece."

Ella grinned.

There was only one guest that I cared to see tonight, though.

"Have you seen any...*demigods?*" I asked lightly.

"I have not," Ella answered.

Frustration flashed through me. Perseus had made a comment that all I showed was men, so I'd carved women, too. I *was* an artist, even though I mostly cheated by using the idiots that dared to meet my gaze—even with proper warning. I'd expanded this show just to prove a point to her.

After spending four hours on one set of tits, I would be angry if she didn't show up.

"I'm ready," I said curtly, moving past Ella.

My heels clicked on the stone steps as I went to the front doors of the museum. The guards there promptly opened them for me as I plastered on my best smile.

Madeline was a woman of the world. She was beautiful, fun, sexy, alluring. She was a siren that drew everyone close to her, an obelisk of light to the moths that collected her work.

That was who I was right now. Not Medusa, not a monster, and most certainly not a mafia boss.

I stepped into the museum foyer, a round room with a high domed ceiling. Patrons turned their attention to me, greeting me as I passed them.

Ella had been right. Mortals filled the museum, their chatter deafening. They met me with admiring gazes and gasps as I made my way toward the exhibit.

I strode into the room. A golden spotlight highlighted all my statues lined up against the black walls.

Most of the male statues were missing their cocks. I'd broken them off, creating different singular pieces of just hard, veiny shafts. I enjoyed overhearing snippets of conversations, masked individuals theorizing which cock belonged to which statue.

"Miss Winters," a man greeted me, giving me a deep bow. His cerulean blue mask almost slid off his face, but he caught it as he rose back up. "This is quite the exhibit."

"Thank you, Mr...?"

"Oh! Mr. Goldberg."

A chairman of the city council. "Mr. Goldberg," I purred. "It's so hard to tell behind the mask, you know."

He let out a boisterous laugh and stepped closer to me. I could smell his fetid breath. He raised a hand, touching my face.

"You are stunning, Miss Winters." His voice trembled in a way that made me want to vomit.

I took a step back, and he took one forward, reaching for me again. I felt a wave of rage, but before I could act on it, a smooth voice interjected.

"There you are."

Percy stepped between the two of us, her elbow shoving him back as she looped her arm in mine. She was wearing a tuxedo, her silver hair slicked back. Her jaw was sharp, her cheekbones high. The masquerade mask she wore could not hide how alluring she was.

"Excuse me, I was having a conversation—"

"My apologies. It appeared to be more of an uninvited groping from an ape," Percy said.

He gawked, and she tightened her grip on me.

"I must steal our beautiful artist," Percy said smoothly. "There is an issue we must attend to. And if you are smart and would like to live to see tomorrow, you will purchase the most expensive piece here and then leave. Understood?"

I was promptly steered away before the bastard could continue.

"Thanks," I said. "He was about to join my collection tonight."

"You know, you could have kicked him in the balls," Percy said. "A mere flick of your finger would have sent him to his knees. He's a weak and pathetic representative of the human species."

"Those moments still startle me," I murmured. "The audacity is astounding."

She was silent as we worked through the crowd. I could feel her anger.

"Don't kill him," I said.

Gazes followed us, whispers as well, but neither of us cared. We were simply two alluring women in their eyes. They didn't know *what* we were. They didn't know that we ruled the city they lived in, that everyone was on our payroll here. That we could end their lives in a blink if we chose to.

"Don't worry about it," she bristled.

"He just joined the council a year ago," I hissed under my breath.

"And? Now he can join the council of the underworld."

"*Percy.*"

She smiled. "You aren't the only serial killer in this city, princess. Besides, why do you care? You're such a hypocrite. You've been murdering for thousands of years, yet you balk at me wanting to kill a man who touched you without your permission."

"What would Orpheus and Theseus think? Your side doesn't just kill. Especially for us monsters."

She shot me a sour look. The two of us stepped into the part of the exhibit where the female statues were. It was quieter in this room and slightly less crowded.

She shoved me to the side, pinning me against a wall that was just out of sight. "Why did you invite me if you were just going to bring up the line that divides us?"

"I didn't think you were coming," I said. I ignored the heat I felt being so close to her.

"I told you I bought tickets months ago," she growled.

"And?" I quipped.

She scoffed and turned around, stealing two glasses of champagne off a tray from a meandering waiter that passed us, handing me one of them.

"I'm not drinking—"

"Save your lies," she snapped, clearly irritated.

We both tipped back our glasses. She turned, surveying the room. "You carved these?"

"I did," I said, my stomach fluttering. I didn't need her approval, but I still enjoyed hearing her thoughts. Even if she was a demigod.

"Show me the tits," she insisted.

I felt a streak of pride as I led her towards a statue of a

woman at the very end. She was curvy, with soft biteable rolls and plush thighs that I wanted to lick. And her breasts. They were stunning.

We simply stared, drinking in silence.

"Okay," she said after a few moments. "You were right. Those are great tits."

I smirked over the edge of my champagne flute. "I have a good eye."

"You do," she chuckled. "I'm glad you added more variety to your show. You really outdid yourself, Mads."

"Careful," I said. "That almost sounds like a compliment."

We both went back to sipping our drinks in silence.

It wasn't that I hated her. I certainly didn't. In fact, Percy was the only other immortal in the entire world that I'd ever tolerated. One might even say we were friends, but I'd never dared to admit that.

"You know who she reminds me of?" Percy asked.

"Who?"

"That nun. The one from a couple hundred years ago."

I snorted, feigning innocence. "I don't know the one you speak of."

"Oh, come on," Percy laughed. "You know exactly who I'm talking about. I found you fucking her at a convent in Spain."

"I don't know what you're talking about," I sniffed.

"The year was 1556."

"Percy, that's way more than a couple hundred years ago. I thought you could count better than that."

She ignored me, continuing. "King Philip II was ruling. They sent me to check on a new convent and I found you on the altar, fucking her with your tail. She thought you were a demon, but she certainly didn't seem to care. Probably the closest that woman ever got to heaven."

"Percy," I hissed, flushing. I glanced to my left and right, shaking my head. "There might have been *inspiration* drawn from a past lover."

"Mmhmm," Percy hummed. "*Inspiration.*"

"What were you even doing there? As a woman?"

"Oh, I cut off all my hair and pretended to be a man," Percy snorted. "I have the strength of ten of them. They didn't argue."

Back to our comfortable silence. We stared at Sister Mary's tits for another few minutes before moving on to the next piece.

Percy let out a low whistle.

"You're terrible," I teased.

"I can be," she snickered.

I stared at her for a moment, my heartbeat quickening. Her scent hit me, and I felt my mouth water.

Fuck. *Not now.*

There had been many times over the years that I'd felt this around her, but it was ridiculous. A hunger that could not be slaked, an emptiness which nothing could fill.

Damn demigods.

"I need to go," I said sharply. "And check on other patrons. Enjoy the show."

She frowned as I left her abruptly. I heard her call my name, but I fled. I needed to get away.

My heart thrashed in my chest as I shoved through the crowd, leaving the exhibit and almost running for a quieter space.

I slipped into a room full of paintings, the scent of oil and linen faint but present. I let out a breath, my heart still thundering. Blood rushed to my ears.

There was something wrong with me when I was with her. But there was something even more wrong when I wasn't.

"Fuck," I whispered.

Why was I thinking about this now?

"Is there something wrong, *Medusa*?"

I spun around just as a blade glinted, a man moving close in a dark blur and burying it straight into my stomach. I gasped, pain spearing me as he drove it in and twisted, catching me against him.

"It's time one of *you* died," he whispered. "This is for your betrayal."

"Ryan?" I rasped.

My vision was dimming. The weapon wasn't ordinary, not the kind that I would normally heal from.

Orpheus' blade.

He yanked it free and shoved me back. I stumbled, hitting the wall hard enough that it rattled. Several paintings fell, crashing to the ground.

Pain seared my veins as I sucked in harsh breaths. I felt like I had thousands of wasps buzzing in my blood, it was excruciating. I fell to my knees. "What are you doing?" I rasped.

The Minoan Bull, who we all called Ryan, regarded me coldly, his eyes searing me with hatred. His form flickered from that of a man to his true, monstrous form—wavering back and forth. The magic he was using to disguise himself was clearly borrowed and draining quickly.

"Who are you working for?" I rasped.

I recognized when someone was doing a task. I knew that look all too well.

"You abandoned me," he said, glowering.

"They locked you up," I rasped. "How did you get the blade?"

Orpheus' knife was deadly to monsters like me. The Colchian Dragon had been stabbed with it before, but the Fates had interfered.

Clearly, they would not do so now.

He let out a dark chuckle. "Should have stayed that way. But no worries, Medusa. I have taken my vengeance and will be out of your lives. I only needed to stab you to set in motion the events they wanted to happen. Who knows," he said, smirking. "Maybe they'll even ask me to join your mafia."

"*Who?*" I rasped.

I couldn't speak anymore. I heard him walk away. Leaving me alone to die.

Who? Who wanted this?

Fuck.

This wasn't supposed to be how I went. I wasn't supposed to die at the hands of some lousy bullheaded bastard, I was supposed to go out being suffocated between a lover's sweet thighs.

This was fucking ridiculous.

My head fell back, and I stared at the ceiling, at the ugly museum lights. I could feel my immortality slipping between my fingertips, bleeding from me, drawing me closer to death.

Percy.

The worst part about dying was realizing I wouldn't make it to our Sunday brunch. Instead of virgin mimosas with Percy, she'd be burying me—and all without either of us ever sharing anything aside from a single kiss.

I regretted it all.

CHAPTER 3

ELEKTRA

P ercy

I rapped my knuckles as hard as I could on the door to the house, glancing over my shoulders at the clouds of smoke coming from the town. I could even hear the screams from here.

I'd tried. I'd tried so hard to stop the madness and I had failed. Again. How could I call myself a hero?

I hated this. I had been alive for so long and had forgotten the brutality of mortals and men.

I knocked harder, sending up a silent prayer that it would be a woman's home. I would have to take her clothing and horses in the stables—

The door flew open. I turned my head and froze.

Her eyes.

"Medusa?" I rasped.

She hissed, baring sharp fangs. She had the face of a young

woman, but I knew her eyes. Golden with snake irises. She wore
a dress, a black pendant laying against her breasts. "Perseus?!"

"What in the devil's name are you doing in the colonies?"

"ME? What are you doing here?"

"They think I'm a witch, Medusa."

"It's Mary now," she snarled. She pushed her head out,
looking towards the smoke. "Call me Mary. I swear the mortals
have gone backwards. Did you know that if you were anyone else
in the world, you would be a statue right now?"

"Mary, Margaret, Medusa—I don't give a fuck what you call
yourself. Let me in," I begged. "I need to hide."

"Absolutely not. If we're discovered, we'll both burn."

"Please forgive me, but last time we met, a mere gaze from
you could turn beings to stone. As you just mentioned. Is that not
still true?"

"It is. Still don't know why you're immune," she muttered.

"This is my favor. I helped you out last time when Queen
Elizabeth wanted your head."

She pinched her face and grabbed me by my collar, tugging
me in. "Damn favors. Damn it all. The gods and Fates have
forsaken us. I just finished decorating this house, Perseus."

She slammed the door behind me and then shoved me against
it, her hands warm on my body. My breath hitched, all of my
thoughts simply leaving me as her lips nearly touched mine.

"If you try anything strange, demigod, I will kill you."

I leaned forward out of instinct despite her threat, our lips
touching. She gasped against me, but I couldn't stop myself. I
hadn't been touched in so long. She moaned against me, her fangs
tugging my bottom lip, piercing me.

The taste of venom filled my mouth, but it was sweet. My
mouth tingled, my cunt aching with need.

She yanked back with a hiss.

"You whore," she growled. "I hate demigods. You disgust me. Never do that again."

I blushed. "I'm sorry," I whispered. "I forgot myself."

She turned, her back facing me. I looked away from her, not knowing why I had done that.

Why had I just kissed a monster?

"You owe me two favors for this," she said. "Since you kissed me."

"Deal," I whispered.

It was a price I didn't mind paying.

———

Mortals were jam-packed in the exhibit like a can of sardines. I was proud of how many came just to see her art. I squeezed out into the round foyer of the museum, scowling. Madeline had disappeared in such a rush, and part of me felt the need to apologize.

I had done nothing wrong. Right?

I replayed our conversation through my mind, mentally noting that I still needed to take care of Mr. Goldenberry or whatever the fuck his name was. I would have Diego take him to one of our clubs. He and Eric could warm him up for me.

A dark figure passed by, drawing my gaze.

I scowled. He looked familiar.

His form flickered, and I felt my stomach drop.

The bull. The Minoan Bull. Jason had done a lot of shit in his life, but locking that bastard up had been a good thing.

"Hey!" I yelled.

He paused, turning. He stood a few feet from me, his shoulders tense and burning eyes reminding me of death. "Be glad, demigod," he growled. "It was her and not you."

My stomach flipped. He left, rushing towards the museum doors.

It was her and not you.

Madeline.

"No," I whispered, panic washing over me.

I turned, looking around wildly. I took off running, letting my instincts lead me.

"Madeline!" I shouted.

I went down a hallway, shoving people out of the way, listening for any signs of her. I knocked into a waiter, a plate of glasses crashing to the floor.

I ran past a room and then doubled back, noting the paintings on the floor. I rushed inside, falling to my knees as I came to her.

Madeline was on the floor, her blood spreading around her in a dark pool. She would be pissed that her dress was ruined.

I pulled her into my lap. "Hey," I said, patting her face. "Mads. Wake up." My fingers ran down her body, feeling where the wound was. It was just a knife wound. Her blood coated my hand now, chilling me. "Mads," I said again, more insistent this time. *Fuck.*

Why wasn't she moving?

I leaned down, pressing my ear against her chest.

Her heart was barely beating.

"*Mads,*" I whispered.

Panic ran through me again. A knife wound should not have done this to her. She was an ancient monster, one that had survived many blades.

For the first time since I had known her, I had the very real notion that I might have to face tomorrow without her.

And that simply would not do.

"Hang on, you stupid bitch," I whispered, lifting her. "Out

of all the ways you could go dying on me, the Minoan Bull was the last one I expected. You are better than him."

My muscles coursed with energy and I rushed her through the museum, leaving a trail of red behind. I burst out into the chilly night, lifting my gaze to the sky. I slung her over one of my shoulders and brought my fingers to my lips, ignoring the taste of blood that met my tongue and the strange rush that followed it. I blew a low whistle, watching as my trusty steed came towards me as a sleek motorcycle.

It was times like this I wondered what the mortals saw. Did they see a motorcycle driving itself towards me, weaving through the cars like they didn't exist? Did they see a rider?

I wasn't sure. It came to a stop in front of me, the tires screeching on the pavement.

My pegasus. One that could morph into what I needed at the moment, which was typically a motorcycle.

Right now, I needed their wings. Their body changed into their original form, a silver horse with wings that stretched at least ten feet each. The feathers reflected the city lights, smoke curling from their nostrils.

I had two gifts from the gods, which were more than the other demigods could say. One was my lightning bolt, my only gift from Zeus. The other was Elektra, a gift from Hephaestus after I'd helped him rid his home of Hades' demons.

There were monsters, and then there were actual pests. Those demons had fallen into the second category.

I swung my leg over Elektra, taking a seat. Madeline's heart was growing fainter as I seated her, pulling her legs around my waist and holding her to my body. Her blood coated us, the rage of panic never-ending.

"Take us to the Hydras, Elektra," I rasped. "As fast as you can."

They were the only beings I knew that might help.

I held Madeline as Elektra lifted into the sky, closing my eyes and breathing in her scent. Listening to her faint heartbeat.

My chest felt like a blade had been driven clean through. I was confused, panicked, and scared. I would fight the Fates for her soul if I needed to.

I could not lose her.

I wasn't ready.

We had brunch on Sunday.

We had a Friday dinner in Athens next month.

A holiday show at the end of the year that no one else had been interested in, so naturally I'd invited her since she appreciated the arts.

Fuck.

Madeline was my only friend.

"Stay alive," I whispered. "Please. We can make it."

Within a few minutes, Elektra skidded to a halt in front of the grand doors of the mansion on the cliffs outside Moirai. The sound of the ocean crashing against them matched the rushing of my blood as I slid off the bike, carrying Madeline up the marble steps.

The door flew open, Bash stepping out. Bash was one of three Hydra men, and arguably the smartest of the bunch.

He pushed his glasses up the bridge of his nose, glowering at me. "You can't just show up unannounced, demigod. What the fuck are you doing here? And what's wrong with *her*?"

"She's hurt," I wheezed, carrying her past him.

"Percy—"

"Get Argos," I snarled at him. "Medusa is dying."

Bash stared for a moment, his green eyes filled with disbelief. "Impossible."

"GET ARGOS!" I shouted.

I carried her inside, my knees giving way. I laid her out on the cold floor of their entryway, hovering over her.

Her body began to slowly morph. Golden serpents replaced her long brown hair, her skin covered with glittering bronze scales. Her legs became a lower serpentine half, her tail long and unmoving. Leathery, umber wings stretched behind her, blood dripping from the tips.

None of the snakes made a noise. They weren't even moving.

Her chest rose and fell in the shallowest of breaths.

"Mads," I whispered. "You can't fucking die. This isn't fair."

"Percy."

I looked up as Argos stepped in. Behind him were Pierce and Bash. His white brows pulled together, his lips pressing into a fine line.

"Why are you here?"

"She's been stabbed, and she's not healing," I said. "It was the Minoan Bull, but I think it was Orpheus' blade. The one that was stolen."

Argos shook his head and knelt next to her, touching the knife wound in her stomach. He pressed lightly, green puss oozing out. My stomach roiled, and I fought the urge to vomit.

"If it is indeed his blade, then I don't think there is hope," he said, pushing and prodding the wound. He let out a soft hum. "This is unfortunate. Medusa is one of us."

I snarled, tears blurring my vision. "I have never asked you for help. I need you to heal her."

He snorted and leaned back on his heels. "Why do you care? It has always been you against us, right? The demigods against us *unworthy* creatures. It doesn't matter that the three of us could gut the daughter of Zeus here and now. That the demigods are outnumbered. You still see yourself as better."

I fought the urge to slap him. I wanted to so fucking bad that my knuckles whitened as my fingers curled into fists. I could feel the buzz of electricity in my veins, the power yearning to be wielded.

"I'm not asking you to heal her, *Hydra*," I gritted out. My voice became icy, stoic. If I kept showing my emotions, they would push back harder. "I'm *telling* you to heal her. If you cannot, then I will personally see to your destruction."

Pierce and Bash both growled, but Argos held up a hand. "She is one of us. We will help. But you must leave, Percy, as you are not. If this was truly the bull's doing, and not yours, then bring him to us. I will call the others. He will face consequences from us all. And tell your Orpheus that we have found his blade."

Fuck Orpheus and his blade. "I'm *not* leaving her."

"I'm not *asking*," he returned. Argos was cold, his voice lacking any emotion. His appearance seemed to reflect that, his pale skin coupled with icy white hair. There was a scar that ran down the left side of his face.

That was something all three Hydras had in common. Their scars.

"I'm telling you to leave, Perseus. We cannot heal her with you here. Go."

I was unmoving, but they didn't give me a choice. Pierce stepped over her and grabbed me by my jacket, hauling me back and throwing me outside.

My ass hit their top step, and he shook his head, mumbling as he slammed the front door behind him.

I sat there for a few moments, holding the tears in. Holding my emotions in.

She would be okay.

She had to be.

For centuries, we'd never missed an appointment. She certainly couldn't start now. She wasn't allowed to just because she got stabbed by a stupid knife.

I drew in a shaky breath, looking at my hands.

Perhaps I would have spared the mortal man's life tonight, but after everything that had happened, that would not be the case. I reached into my suit pocket and pulled out my phone, dialing Diego's number.

"Yes, Mistress?"

"Diego," I said, wiping away the rest of my tears. "We're going hunting. Pick me up outside the Hydra mansion."

"Yes, Mistress."

I was going to make that human piece of shit regret ever breathing in Madeline's presence, and then I was going to hunt down the Minoan Bull and end him. Jason had been a fool for simply locking that monster away.

Until his soul crossed the River Styx, I would hunt him.

Only then, would I be satisfied.

CHAPTER 4

MORTAL BLOOD

P ercy

The building vibrated with club music. Only a few floors above me, one of my clubs teemed with dancing bodies, laughter, and drinks. Moirai never stopped, even on a night like tonight, where everything was going wrong.

Down here, it felt like the Underworld. The basement was cold with stained gray walls, a place of death. I could almost hear the whispers of Charon here.

Diego and Eric waited diligently for my signal, their expressions unreadable. The two floors above us were heavily guarded by more of my men, protected from the outside world.

I dragged Mr. Goldberg by his hair down the steps, enjoying his futile whimpers. He clawed at my hand, trying desperately to break free. But he was just a human.

A mere mortal.

I could feel the darkness consuming me. The rage. The

hate. The anger. Electricity ran through my veins, my power consuming me.

The monsters hated me. The demigods hated me. The gods hated me. And perhaps the Fates did too.

"I have money," he gasped. "*Please.* I haven't done anything wrong."

I tossed him forward. His body hit the floor with a heavy thud. Behind him, there was a metal chair that was bolted down, chains waiting next to it.

"Chain him," I commanded.

I stood still as Diego and Eric grabbed Mr. Goldberg. They dragged him into the chair, his kicking and screaming trivial.

For a moment, I thought about having him stripped. I could. I mulled it over as they chained him to the chair, his screams of protests drowned out by my thoughts.

I'd leave his clothes on. It would make the cleanup easier.

They fastened the last of the chains around his ankles. He was bound now, his eyes darting back and forth.

"I'm sure you're feeling a lot of panic right now," I said, stepping closer to him. I studied him, unable to stop my smile. "It doesn't feel good, does it?

His expression soured. "Fuck you," he growled. "You stupid whore. I don't know what you want, but you won't get it from me."

"Tell me, have you ever done something to a woman before? Hurt her? Raped her? The way you grabbed Madeline tonight was very *comfortable.* You're used to getting what you want, aren't you?"

His face paled, eyes darting back and forth. Sweat dripped from him, his stench disgusting me. "I don't know what you're talking about."

"Okay then, we'll start with your fingers. Once you confess all of your dirty little sins, maybe I'll make the pain stop. And just know that I'm the last face you'll ever see in your miserable life. Say your prayers to your god, because I am your end."

His eyes widened as I lifted my hand. My bolt appeared, hissing against my palm. It was bright enough that it cast a soft blue glow through the room, its warmth spreading through me.

"What are you?!" he screeched.

"A hero." I lowered the sharp tip of the bolt to his fingers.

It cut through like butter. His screams echoed around me as I severed the fingers on his left hand, watching as they hit the floor. He yanked and pulled; the chains jingling. My bolt was hot enough that it cauterized the skin, no blood dripping.

"Tell me," I said again. "Tell me all the things you've done, little man."

And he did.

I lost track of time as I listened to him confess. His words were vile, his stories making me sick. It wasn't the first time, nor would it be the last.

Half-way through the interrogation, I'd switched to a knife. It trembled in my hand as I watched his soul go.

Hades would have fun with that one.

Perhaps he would be taken to the Pyriphlegethon river. It would be a special type of hell for someone like him.

"The damned ghosts in torments fry," I cited.

Blood dripped down onto the floor, pooling at my feet. I let out a breath, watching as his body slumped in the chair. I stared at his frozen, terrified expression.

Only a few hours ago, he'd been so god damned smug when groping Madeline.

Men like him made me sick.

I didn't regret killing him.

"Clean this up," I said, looking up at Diego and Eric.

"Yes, Mistress."

They stepped forward, the two of them already working in tandem.

Killing that man hadn't soothed me the way it normally might have. I let out a sigh and turned, going back up the steps to the door. I went out into the hallway, stretching my arms.

"Mistress."

I turned, meeting Diego's gaze.

"I can get you new clothes."

I looked down at myself. Blood stained my clothes, but I didn't care. I was numb inside, nothing pleasing me. "I'm not done hunting tonight," I said. "There will be more blood."

He winced, although he did his best to hide it. "The humans will notice..."

Annoyance flitted through me, but I nodded. "I'll be in my office and then I'll be gone. After you and Eric finish cleaning, you can take the rest of the night off."

Diego gave a curt nod, although he clearly wasn't pleased. I didn't care. He was my second in command because he knew how to keep his fucking mouth shut.

I left him and went down the hall, all of my thoughts returning to Madeline. What if she died?

The Minoan Bull's head would be mine.

I made my way to the elevator, passing three men that stood guard. I pressed the button and stepped inside, taking it to the top floor.

Every building that I owned had an office for me in case I needed it. My faction of the Three Fates Mafia worked differently from the others. It was less about a specific area that belonged to me, and more about the amount of real estate I owned. Each branch that controlled a part of the city still had let me buy buildings. Even the monsters.

I preferred to be spread out. It helped me eliminate the turf wars that happened between them. I didn't have those problems. I still made the same amount of money, maintained influence, but all with less of a headache.

I used my power for good. There were many parts of the city that I had used my money to improve, to help the mortals that constantly made their world hell.

I took the elevator up to the office floor and pulled out my phone. I called Argos for the fifth time since I'd left Madeline with the Hydras, only to be sent to voicemail again.

"Fuckers," I muttered.

If they didn't answer me soon, then I'd end up breaking into their mansion. But not until I hunted down the bull.

Not until I killed him for touching her.

———

Forty-eight hours.

That was how long I'd been awake.

That was how long I'd been tracking the Minoan Bull.

That was how long I'd been failing to find him.

I'd scoured all of Moirai. Turned over every stone in every territory. Threatened everyone I could. It had done nothing for me. Madeline was still in the Hydra's mansion and the only update I'd gotten was 'she'll live'. All of my other messages were left unanswered.

Ryan was still missing.

I was slowly, but surely, falling apart.

Killing that man hadn't been enough. There was a dark thirst building within, one that death wasn't quenching.

I needed her to be okay. Her wellness was a plague to me. They'd told me she'd live, but was that enough?

My leg moved up and down in a constant rhythm as I checked my watch. My stomach twisted as people moved outside the grand windows of the restaurant, the skies gray as colder weather gripped us. The lack of sleep was wearing on me, but I had decided that I should come here, anyway.

It was Sunday. She never missed the appointments we made.

Through the centuries, through wars that razed civilizations, and being women in a man's world, we still always found each other. Intentionally or unintentionally.

My gaze moved from the windows back to the ceiling. I liked this place because the decor was ornate, the tiles above us gilded. The molding was gold as well, and there was a mural at the center of Aphrodite emerging from the sea.

"Ma'am, it's been over an hour. Are you certain you aren't ready to order yet?"

Fuck. I'd already been sitting here for an hour.

I clenched my jaw and looked up at the waiter. It wasn't their fault that Madeline hadn't shown up for our Sunday brunch. There had been a small, very hopeful part of me that had believed she would.

That she'd come through the front doors, call me an idiot for even thinking she might die, and order champagne for breakfast.

I drew in a soft breath, forcing myself to speak in an even tone. "I'll have a...virgin mimosa."

Their confusion was momentary. "Do...do you mean orange juice?"

"A virgin mimosa," I said again. I gripped the edge of the table, my heart beating a little faster. That's what Madeline called it the other day, so that's what it was.

They winced and nodded. "Right away, ma'am."

They scurried off, leaving me alone. *Relax.* My shoulders melted, and I made myself take a deep breath. I still felt rage. I still felt fear.

Being ignored pissed me off. The night that the Bull had

stabbed Madeline, he'd somehow disappeared into the under-belly of the city. It was as if he had vanished.

No one had any information.

The cameras hadn't been helpful.

The police had been useless.

She'll live. I was holding onto that. It was the only thing keeping me sane.

Since Friday night, I had come to terms with several things. One, I was friends with her. She was my oldest friend, in fact, and we'd been lying to ourselves for centuries.

It was no longer a crime for a demigod to love a monster. That was the other thing I'd finally let myself realize.

She wasn't just my friend.

Perhaps it had been the taste of her blood that I'd had, but I was slowly going mad. My need for her persisted, but with an added fear of never being able to fulfill my secret desires.

Maybe I'd wasted centuries.

We'd been doing each other favors since we'd met long ago. Helping each other make it through the rises and falls of humanity, two relics that belonged in another world. A hero and a villain. A monster and a beautiful woman.

I was the monster, not her.

I needed to know if she felt the same way. If she didn't, then I would accept it. But the idea of never finding out made me regret everything. I'd gone through every memory of her, picking them apart, screaming at myself about how I'd been so blind.

I raked my fingertips through my silver hair, glancing up as the waiter brought me a flute of orange juice.

She wasn't coming.

For the first time in over two thousand years, Madeline had missed our date.

They'd told me she was alive, but now I doubted that completely. Because if she was alive, she would be here.

"That's all I'm getting."

The waiter furrowed their brows. "It's on the house. I've seen you and your wife before. Is she okay?"

My *wife*. Even this mortal had seen what I had not. My throat felt like it was closing in.

"I don't know," I whispered.

They nodded. "I hope to see you both again."

They left me. I stared at the orange juice, fighting back tears again.

I was a fool.

"You're looking very sad, Perseus. I almost pity you."

I turned in my chair, my stomach twisting as a beautiful woman walked towards me. She wore crimson lipstick and a black dress, her hair pulled back into a chignon. She came to my table, sliding into the seat that was meant for Madeline.

"Clotho."

My voice was faint, cold sweat icing my neck.

"Perseus," she said, raising a brow.

"What can I do for you, madam? I have not seen you in person since..."

"Since the day you left for Medusa's shore and failed your first mission." Her voice was neither warm nor cool.

The Fates rarely visited anyone in person, even when forming the Three Fates Mafia. It unnerved me to be face to face with Clotho.

"I failed, but I do not regret that failure."

She let out a soft *hmm*, her smile making me feel queasy. "Indeed, your destiny changed that day. I much prefer this one to the other. Monsters and demigods walk this world still because we deem it so. And there is fresh blood from the gods themselves. Some might see what we are doing as kind, others will consider it an affront against previous agreements."

"Are you here to kill me, then?" I asked. "Jason and Hercules are dead. Ashley and Serena have taken their place in our world. They are fledglings, but they are fierce. Am I to be replaced?"

"No," she answered. "You ask me too many questions. I will only allow two more in this conversation."

I tensed as she snapped her fingers. A black envelope appeared on the table, a golden wax stamp gleaming with the Three Fates Mafia sigil.

"Open it," she said.

I felt nauseous as I took the envelope. I broke the seal, wondering what fate I had just opened for myself.

"No email this time?" I chuckled.

"That counts as another question. And no. No email."

Fuck. No more questions. I clenched my teeth as I pulled out the manilla piece of paper, unfolding it.

Dear Perseus, daughter of **Zeus**,
Congratulations, your mate has been found. Unfortunately, she only has ONE month to live. We, the Fates, have notified you so that you may make better life decisions.
P.S. she's always been your mate
Clotho, Lachesis, and Atropos
Three Fates Mafia

Everything inside me went numb. Every word was a punch to the gut. The question slipped out of me before I could stop myself. "Why?"

"She was saved, but her threads are ending. It is her time. You have known she was your mate for centuries, Perseus. And yet you've done nothing about it. I don't pity you." Clotho stood up, her eyes searing me. "The gods deemed you a failure the moment you refused to kill her. And all for what? So you could pine over her until her death? What a sad ending for another sad hero."

Before I could respond, she disappeared, leaving me alone.

My hand trembled, my thoughts racing. Our history was a long one. It couldn't just end.

This couldn't be the end.

I pulled out my phone and hit Argos' number again, my knuckles turning white as it went to voicemail again.

Fuck it. I was going back to their house. They'd let me in.

I had to see her.

CHAPTER 5

TWO TRUTHS AND A LIE

M adeline

My eyes slowly opened. I blinked a few times until I realized I was wearing sunglasses. My body was unmoving, lethargic. My gut ached.

"What. The. Fuck."

Someone had done something to me. My thoughts felt foggy as I lifted my head, looking around the room. Panic washed through me. I had many enemies, several of which would bind me like this.

My gut twisted. There was no way it was the *goddess*. No way it was anyone like her...

I didn't recognize it, but the scent was familiar.

Monster.

Hydra.

I relaxed. I was gonna kill them. Whoever had handled me this way would meet a rocky ending as soon as I saw them.

I looked down at myself again and frowned. Why was I in my monster form?

My eyes closed, and I reached for the ability to change, to shift. But nothing happened.

The door opened. Bash stepped inside, confirming my suspicions.

"Excellent. You're finally awake. This means I won my bet. Argos and Pierce thought you would die."

"If you don't bring me my things right now, I will kill you," I growled.

Bash snorted as he plopped in the chair next to the bed he tied me down to.

"You should be dead right now," Bash said, studying me like I was a specimen. "And you should thank us for saving you. To be fair, we owe you some favors. I think your life will cancel all of them, correct?"

"Wrong." This son of a bitch. The moment I could, I would break his jaw.

"Your life is only worth one favor?"

"The shit I've done for the three of you snakes? Yes. Now, untie me."

"I can't. Not until your wound completely heals. It's been slow progress, Medusa. Slower than it should be for a monster. I am concerned for you."

I hated him. I hated everyone. And I especially hated being bound to a bed by three men who fancied themselves gods.

"Bash, *honey*." I gave him a fanged smile. "If you don't let me up, your death will be slow and painful. I need a cup of coffee, a cigarette, and a piss."

He sighed. "You are severely injured, Madeline. You almost died."

"We don't simply *die*," I chastised. My memories were

coming back to me now. The Minoan Bull, the art show, the knife. "Ian was stabbed with that knife and he was fine."

"He has two hearts." Bash shrugged. "And your body has not reacted the same way. That blade is cursed, if it is the one that belongs to Orpheus. It can kill *anything* if used in a fatal area. Perseus still has problems with her thigh, I'm certain."

"I'm still alive," I snapped.

"What's the last thing that you remember? And what day do you think it is?"

I glowered at him as I thought about the show again. I was pissed that I had been so rudely interrupted.

That *motherfucking* Minoan Bull was now on my kill list. The monsters that were left in this world did our best not to kill each other, but he had crossed the line.

Percy.

"What day is it?" I suddenly whispered.

"It's Sunday."

Fuck. Gods damn it all. "What time?" I was already trying to sit up. Pain speared my stomach, my muscles protesting.

"It's already 3 P.M.," Bash said. "You're not getting out of the restraints. Not in your condition."

"I didn't ask for your help. In fact, I don't know who thought bringing me to you was a good idea, but it was not. I need to leave. I've missed an important appointment."

"It was the best idea," he argued. "We have a..." He trailed off. "Never mind. We helped heal you. Not even the Fates could have done that."

"Alright, well, now you are for sure a moron," I sighed, plopping my head back on the pillows. "As if you are stronger than the Fates."

"We create our own destiny," he said, his voice harsh.

I looked at him, wishing that my sunglasses were off so I

could turn him to stone. I tried to change back to Madeline, knowing that form could slip through these ropes.

Nothing happened.

Again.

The snakes around my head hissed at Bash in unison, every fiber of my being disliking him right now. My long lower half stretched out, tied every few inches. Scales glimmered, reminding me I was a hideous creature.

I opened my mouth to argue with him again, when the sound of growls and shouts interrupted me. Bash stood as the door burst open. The room filled with a flash of light.

Percy stood in the doorway holding her lightning bolt and a pitcher of orange juice. The air buzzed with electricity, her silver hair floating around her with the static charge.

"What are you doing?" Bash snarled.

"I have an appointment with Madeline," Percy said, her voice cold despite the heat in her gaze. She was looking at me, only at me.

My heart raced. I swallowed hard as she came into the room, undoing the ropes that bound me with the touch of her godly weapon. Bash hissed and reached for her, but a sharp command interrupted.

"Let them leave." Argos stood in the doorway with a heavy glower. "Madeline, you owe us one for saving your life. You should have died. I think it's time you go home."

"Agreed," I said sourly.

"She can't even sit up by herself," Bash argued. "You brought her here to have her healed. We've been ignoring you for a reason, demigod."

"You're the one that brought me here?" I hissed.

"I'm the one that found you," she said. "You were very hurt."

I fought the urge to roll my eyes. I couldn't have been that hurt. I was a monster. Someone who had fought countless humans and demigods, had lived for centuries, was resourceful and resilient.

"How will you get her out of here?" Bash snorted.

"I will carry her," Percy said. Her bolt disappeared with the flick of her slender hand, and she set the pitcher of orange juice down on the side table next to the bed.

"You're not strong enough," Bash argued. "You're just a woman."

Percy ignored him as she leaned down. I hesitated for a moment, but then reached for her as she slid her arms beneath my back and hips. Her scent washed over me, one that made my mouth water.

One that had a lingering stain of blood.

"Who did you kill?" I whispered.

She let out a husky chuckle as she lifted me, carrying me past the two glaring Hydra men. "Who didn't I kill? I've been busy since the show Friday night."

A shiver of pleasure worked through me. "Did you get the bull?"

"Not yet."

"I didn't realize Percy was your *pet*, Medusa," Argos said as we passed. There was blood speckling his pale skin, his eyes tracing the two of us in an almost reptilian way. There was an undercurrent of dark malice, one that made my spine stiffen.

"If I weren't feeling like shit, I'd turn you to stone," I growled at him. "Percy is not my *pet*."

He was silent, his gaze following us as Percy marched down the hall. My tail dragged behind, my wings tucked close around us. Part of me wanted to shield her from prying eyes. The Hydras did not forget slights against them, and I worried about what Percy had done.

This house was full of cold marble, impersonal, and exactly

what I would expect from the three of them. It reminded me of Athena's temples from long ago, but it lacked the feminine warmth that had kept those places running.

"I don't know how you will get me home," I murmured to her. "I can't shift right now."

"Don't worry," she said with ease. "I have everything planned. I'll get you home, Mads."

My throat felt like it was closing up. I held onto her, amazed at her strength as she carried me in my monster form—tail, wings, snakes and all—like I weighed no more than a child.

Hydra guards glared as she carried me through the front lobby. Percy stepped through a pool of fresh blood, uncaring as we went out the front door. A car waited at the end of the steps, the skies eerily gray.

One of Percy's men stepped out and opened the door. She lowered me into the backseat, the two of us pushing my long tail inside as well. It took a moment to pile everything inside, and instead of going around to the other side to get in—Percy climbed in and straddled my lap.

"Percy," I whispered.

The door slammed shut. There was a divider between the back and the front so that we couldn't be seen or heard.

She gripped my face as the car drove, tipping my chin up.

"What are you doing?" I rasped. "What are you..."

She leaned down, her eyes flickering luminous blue as her lips met mine.

This wasn't our first kiss, but it was the first one I didn't fight. I was weak right now, but that didn't stop me from reaching up and knotting my taloned fingers into her silver hair, our tongues meeting in desperation. In hunger.

Something had changed.

Something had broken.

She kissed me deeper, her grip tightening as she devoured

me. I groaned against her, butterflies erupting in my stomach as she took me.

Finally, she pulled back to breathe, her cheeks flushed pink.

Normally, I would yell at her or protest about her even touching me. Right now, I couldn't find the will to do so. Her touch was comforting, enthralling. The look on her face reminded me of a hungry beast that was finally released for a hunt.

She wasn't letting me go.

"All this time. We've known each other for centuries and I've known you were mine. I let others rule our lives. I let them divide us. I pretended to be your enemy, pretended to hate you, pretended to want to kill you and *gods damn it*, Madeline." Tears sprang to her eyes. "I saw Clotho."

Those three words sent a chill through me. "Clotho?"

"They gave me a letter."

"What are you talking about? Why would they give you a letter—"

"They said that you're my mate. But I knew. I've always known."

I stared at her for a moment, startled. Hearing those words aloud, the ones that I had done my best to ignore for so long—it felt like I had suddenly spoken my biggest secret into existence.

That the woman holding my face right now was mine.

That all this time I'd been pretending I didn't want her when, in reality, she was the only person in the world I ever cared to please.

"No," I whispered. "We can't."

"Why? Because you're a monster and I'm a demigod? Haven't we seen the others finally get their happy ending?"

"No," I said. "We haven't, Percy. We've seen some of us get a happy ending. Haven't you noticed that two of your kind have died? They were fucking bastards and deserved it, but two souls that have been alive almost as long as ours have been sent to the fields. How do we know that the Fates have goodness in store for us? I've never trusted them. Ever since I was turned into this." I gestured at my body. "At least the others were born monsters. I was forced to become one. I know what it's like to not be treated like a creature. Like a villain."

"I never thought of you as those things," she whispered. "And you're beautiful as a monster, Madeline. You are the most beautiful woman I've ever seen in my life, in either form. How can you curse your existence when you're so damn stunning?"

The snakes around my head hissed at her. She ignored them, even as one struck out and bit her hand.

She reached up with the other and pulled my glasses free. I looked away, but her grip tightened on my jaw, her eyes narrowing.

"Look at me," she said.

"No," I snarled.

"Look. At. Me."

A low growl left me, but I submitted, looking up at her. Truly holding her gaze.

"You are mine," she said. "And I'm not letting you go this time. We're not going to just be friends that do favors anymore. And I'm done pretending we don't deserve to be happy."

"You can't make me," I said, but my words had no bite.

"I can right now," she said. "You're weak. You need someone to help you. Someone to care for you."

"I don't need that at all."

"Someone that will remind you that you're not alone. Someone to touch you..."

"Demigods are disgusting."

Her hand slid down to my breast, her thumb barely brushing one of my nipples. Every nerve in my body came to life, a gasp leaving me as it hardened under her precise touch.

"Really? Demigods are *so* gross."

"*Percy.*"

She leaned down, her lips hovering over my nipple. Her eyes lifted, her lashes casting shadows over her sharp cheekbones.

"Should I stop, Mads?"

"No," I whispered.

She smiled victoriously and leaned back. "That's what I thought. We'll resume when I get you in my bed, then."

"You bitch," I muttered, blushing and looking out the window.

She slid off my lap into the seat next to me, her hand slipping into mine. I gave hers a gentle squeeze, still blushing hard. I hated how well she knew me.

"Is that all the letter said?" I asked. "That we are meant to be together?"

"Yes," she said. "And while you are healing, I'm going to hunt down the Minoan Bull and find the blade. The Hydras healed you, but I worry you need something more. We need the knife."

"Fine," I muttered. "Where are we going?"

"To my place," she said.

I stole a glance at her and then looked back out the window. I'd never seen Percy's home before. I wondered what it would be like.

The two of us were very different.

"If it's ugly, then we go to my place," I huffed. "You know I like luxury."

"I know."

"And I like enormous bathtubs and beautiful lingerie and expensive skincare."

"Of course," she chuckled. "Do you really think I don't

enjoy those things? The suits I wear are more expensive than your dresses."

"Okay, but I have very *specific* tastes."

"If you really hate my home that much, then you can redecorate it and make it ours. You can do whatever you want to it."

I fought back a smile. That made me happier than it should. If I had feet right now, I might have even kicked them with glee.

It was absurd, but everything with Percy suddenly felt right.

CHAPTER 6

FIGHT OR FLIGHT

P ercy

I'd lied to her. I didn't like that I'd lied to her, but I couldn't tell her everything that Clotho had said. Not right now.

Not when I finally had Madeline in my home.

In my room.

I laid her out on my bed, propping up the many pillows behind her head and back so that she could sit up. My gaze trailed down her beautiful body to the stab wound on her stomach. The skin was still inflamed, but the infection was gone and the wound had closed up. It was nothing like it had been the first night.

I trailed my fingertips over her skin, gently, as I came to the scales that began at her hips. Her wings shivered, spreading out further behind her.

"I'm sure you're hungry," I said, pulling my hand back. "What would you like to eat?"

"I'm not hungry," she said. "Not yet, anyway. Your home is not as hideous as I expected for a woman who wears cargo pants sometimes."

"Shut up," I chuckled. "I can think of many times you could have used my many pockets. And you know I mostly wear suits."

"Suits with more pockets."

"If I don't have pockets, how am I supposed to live? How do you live?"

"I have someone carry everything for me," she said.

"Hence why I have to have pockets."

She rolled her eyes. "You're insufferable now that you have me trapped in your bed."

"Yes," I said. "So trapped. How are you feeling?"

"Cranky and horny. Like I want to murder someone and have you fuck me."

"We could do both," I proposed.

"Mm, you know my love language."

I swallowed hard, torn between climbing onto the bed and ravaging her and making her eat. I wanted our first time to be romantic, but I was also tired of waiting.

Clotho's words made my heart skip a beat.

"Percy," she said, her tone serious.

I looked up at her, meeting her gaze. I loved that she could look at me, *truly* look at me. She didn't have to fear that I would die right in front of her.

We'd known the truth for so long, but had always ignored it. Pretended that there wasn't a connection, that we couldn't be together.

"What are we doing?"

Her voice was soft. I'd never heard her speak to anyone like this. Everyone in our world feared her. Had always feared her. The monster who turned people to stone, who killed heroes.

She put up walls around herself like I had. Time hardened my heart, but when I was with her, I felt new again.

"I told you," I said, slipping my hand into hers. I lifted it, kissing her soft knuckles. "We have a lot to make up for. I'm not hiding anymore. I will not pretend I don't want you."

"What *do* you want?" she asked, her tone toughening up. I could almost hear the walls going up.

"I want you," I said. "I want you to be mine. I want to love you. I want a life with you. And I want to stop fighting this feeling that has been haunting me since the day I washed up on your shore. What do you want, Madeline?"

She pulled her hand away. "I want you to let me nap."

Her words stung. I stared at her for a moment, trying to ignore the prick of pain.

She raised a brow and then looked away, rolling over onto her side. I heard her breath, knowing that the movement probably hurt. The snakes around her head rested on the pillow, her wing curving around her body.

"Go," she said. "I don't want to talk right now."

"Fine," I said, pressing my lips together. "You can't hide from me, you know. And I know you will not nap."

"You know nothing about me."

"I'm the only one in this world that knows anything about you." I went to the doorway, trying not to laugh at the irony that I was leaving my room. "I care about you, Mads."

She ignored me, her muscles clearly tense. I wavered between concern and absolute frustration. I should have known that I couldn't just sweep her off her feet and expect her to want a relationship.

I stepped out and shut the door. I went to the railing, leaning over and looking down the staircase. This home was outside Moirai. It wasn't as extravagant as the others, but I liked it. I liked it was quiet. It had wood flooring; the walls painted a deep emerald green and decorated with art. It had color and personality and was nothing like the cold hospital feel the Hydra mansion had.

I glanced at my bedroom door again and then left, going downstairs. She would get over her problems.

I would win her over.

I went down the hall to the kitchen, plopping down on the barstool. I sat there for a moment, the silence comforting.

My phone rang in my pocket. I groaned, closing my eyes for a moment. I didn't want to talk to anyone. But, I pulled it out and answered.

"What?" I asked brusquely.

"Mistress, it's Diego."

"I know that. Speak."

"Two of the trails following the Minoan Bull have gone dead. Eric informed me that they both ended in Orpheus' territory. Because his gang is hostile, we wanted to ask permission to wait until it's dark before pursuing anything further."

"Yes," I sighed. I hated Orpheus' men. All of them were criminal bastards. "It's interesting that the paths led to his territory, considering. I will call him. For now, hold back. Keep your ears to the ground. Is there anything else?"

"You have three packages that need to be delivered. I have not opened them yet."

"Who are they from?"

"Two appear to be from a clothing company, and one is unknown."

"Have someone bring them to me. I wouldn't have a mortal open the unknown one."

"Yes, ma'am."

"I'm in the kitchen," I said. "Medusa will be staying here. Caution our men. If they look at her, they will die."

"Of course. I'll remind everyone."

"Thanks, Diego."

"Always my pleasure. There is one other thing."

"Yes?"

He hesitated, but then spoke. "I was supposed to start my vacation tomorrow, but if I need to push it back—"

"No," I said. "Go. I have it on my calendar, and I know you need to see your family."

He breathed out. "Thank you."

"You're welcome. Send the packages. Make sure Eric is briefed."

We ended the call, and I sighed, leaning against the cold counter top. I'd forgotten he was supposed to go on vacation. Hell, I couldn't remember the last time he had.

I was a heartless bitch most of the time, but I enjoyed taking care of my people. Diego and Eric had done everything for me, never questioning me. Although Diego sometimes pushed me, it was never in a disrespectful way.

Even though being a demigod was lonely, I'd surrounded myself with good people. That was why my branch of the mafia flourished. Yes, we murdered. Yes, we stole. But there was a code of conduct, a moral one that we adhered to.

Unlike Orpheus.

I hated talking to him, but I still hit his contact and pressed the call button. It rang a couple times, and then his voice came through.

"Perseus," he said. "To what do I owe the pleasure?"

"Your knife has been found," I said flatly.

"Where is it?" His tone immediately became harsh, desperate.

"I don't have it. The Minoan Bull does. And I am tracking him for other reasons, but the trails have gone cold."

"That bastard," he breathed. "I will find him and I will kill him."

"No. If you find him first, you will bring him to me. He is mine to kill. In exchange, I'll return the blade to you if I find him first."

"Why wouldn't you? Who else would it go to? It is us against *them*, Perseus. A fact that you seem to have forgotten recently. I heard about your little...excursion with Medusa."

"Madeline," I corrected. "She doesn't go by Medusa any longer. And that is none of your business. What is your business is your blade, which is currently in the possession of a monster I want to kill. We have a mutual interest, Orpheus. Play by the rules."

He was silent, and then let out a dark chuckle. "Fine. We'll play together then. What do you want?"

"I want my men to have immunity in your quarter while we hunt. And not just immunity around the building that I own. The entire area."

"Fine," he growled. "In return, I request the ability to question your men."

"No. They are mine."

"If they have information I need, then I should be able to question them. They are just mortals, Perseus. Idiots. It would not be a violent inquiry..."

"I said no. If there is information found, they will give it to me. I will notify you. That is the deal. I'm doing you a favor by even trying, Orpheus."

"Yes. And why is that? Did something happen to *Madeline*?"

My stomach clenched. Had the Hydras told anyone? It was unlike them to betray information about another monster to our side. "No," I said. "Nothing has happened to her. Are we done here?"

"Yes. Just remember that we *both* play by the rules, Perseus." He hung up abruptly.

"Fucker," I muttered.

I shot a text back to Diego about the agreement with Orpheus, and then sighed.

The sound of wood creaking had me turning on the stool.

"Madeline?" I called.

The movement sounded closer to the door.

I rushed from the kitchen to the living room. I made it to the front door right as Madeline reached for the handle.

"Where the fuck are you going?" I snarled.

She paused, letting out an exasperated sigh. Like I was *annoying* her. "I'm leaving."

"You're not going anywhere." I pulled her back from the door, only for her to turn and shove me hard enough that I hit the wall. "You're still hurt!" I yelled.

"I feel much better," she said, opening the door. "Thanks for all the help, but I'm out of here. I have a business to run. No time for emotions."

"You fucking idiot," I growled, rushing towards her.

She moved to the side, and I slammed the door shut, twisting out of the way as she reached for me, her fangs bared. "You bitch," she growled. "I hate you!"

"You don't hate me," I snapped. "You've never hated me."

She glowered, the snakes around her head hissing together. "Let me leave."

"No." I pressed my back against the door. "This is absurd. You're acting like a child throwing a tantrum."

"I'm acting like a prisoner who is being trapped somewhere she doesn't want to be!" she shouted.

We stared at each other for a split second. But then she turned, racing for the kitchen. I ran after her, my frustration melting into a shaky rage as I followed her.

We rounded the corner right as one of my men stepped into

the kitchen holding three packages. He looked up, his eyes widening as he saw her.

"Wow," he whispered. "You're so pretty."

"Madeline, no!" I yelled, drawing my lightning bolt.

It was too late. He'd already looked at her, she'd looked at him. I watched as he froze in place, his skin turning ashen gray as he slowly became stone.

I watched as he died before us, turning into a statue.

CHAPTER 7

SUBMISSION

M adeline

Percy poised her lightning bolt, her eyes burning with anger as we glared at each other. I could see her raw hurt.

It was easier to make her hate me. But she knew that and wasn't letting me win. She wasn't letting me push her away.

"I'm going to leave," I said.

"No."

"I'm not staying."

"You are staying," she snarled. "I will tie you down the way the Hydra did. I will fucking bind you, chain you, and gag you if that's what it takes for you to stop fighting this."

"I have a business to run," I growled, moving closer to her. The air was charged, the heat between us an inferno. "I haven't even called my assistant. I have no idea what my sales were on Friday."

Excuses, excuses, excuses. I was trying to run away, to escape her.

"Do you even need the money? Do you even care?"

"No, but then there was that guy—"

"The one that I gutted?"

My lips parted. Her words were so cold that it startled me. "You killed the councilman?"

"I kidnapped him, chained him, cut off his fingers, and gutted him. And then I hunted for the bull. The one that tried to murder you. I can't find him, but I will." She stepped closer, only a few inches separating us now. The space was unbearable, filled with a canyon of emotions neither one of us seemed to be able to cross. "And when I do, I'm going to do the same fucking thing to him. The only difference is that I'll be mounting his head on my wall like a god damned trophy."

I breathed out. "I can handle my own problems. I will find him myself."

"No. He's mine to kill. I thought you were going to die. You missed our brunch."

"I did," I said, my back straightening. "What do you mean, he's yours to kill? I'm the one with the stab wound."

She grabbed my chin, squeezing hard even as I bared my fangs at her. "I will kill him for you."

I hissed. "*This*. This can't happen."

"Because I'm a demigod?"

"Because we are not destined for a happy ending, Percy!" I shouted, yanking my face from her grip.

Her eyes flickered, the bolt disappearing. "How would you know? You don't know what the Fates have planned for us. We've lived this long."

"Yes, and *look* at us. Look at me," I snapped, gesturing at myself.

I felt a wave of hurt. My words were true, and they stung. I slithered back to the living room, going to her velvet couch. I glowered as I sat down.

Percy had asked me what I wanted and then I'd gotten pissed because I *wanted* to be loved so badly. That's *all* I wanted. For this plague of loneliness to disappear, to finally enjoy another soul. To feel cherished and needed and loved.

There was desire, of course. I wanted that too. But desire had become more of a weapon for me than a gift and sometimes I regretted that. No one ever loved me in this form. I had to become Madeline for that.

"How can you stand here and tolerate me?" I whispered. "Why would you do anything for me? Do you know how many times I've betrayed you over the years? Do you know how many times I've stabbed you in the back?"

"Was it ever because you wanted to or was it because you had to in order to survive?"

Everything I'd ever done had been because I had to survive. I was a cockroach, just like the rest of humanity.

She was quiet for a moment and then came closer to the couch.

"Monsters don't get happy endings, Percy."

"Cerberus and the Colchian did. You can too."

I shook my head. "And what of the gods? They have broken the rules that were put in place for a reason. There is new blood in this world. I don't trust them."

"The gods will protect us," Percy whispered.

"The gods protect no one," I snarled, whipping my head up. Why couldn't she understand that? That they were selfish and used us. A god had turned me into the monster I was. A goddess had used me as her tool for *centuries*. I could feel my venom on my tongue as I spoke. "They certainly never protected someone like me."

"Madeline," Percy whispered. A strand of silver hair had loosened from her bun, her bright blue eyes searching mine.

I'd forgotten how pretty she was.

I'd forgotten how good she was, too.

Percy stepped closer, her movements slow. She lowered down until she was on her knees in front of me. Her hand slid up my chest, up my neck, cupping my jaw. She leaned in, her forehead pressing to mine.

"I've never seen you like this," she whispered. "You've always been in control and you've let no one in. Both of us have survived alone for so long. The Fates have given us their blessing."

"I don't trust those old hags either," I breathed out, bitter. "I don't trust anyone."

"Do you trust me?"

Yes. I swallowed hard, not wanting to say it. But that was the truth.

Any time through the years I had asked her for something, she had done it. Even when it was questionable.

"Yes. Do you trust *me*?"

She nodded. "Even when you're a bitch and do crazy shit like kill one of my men because he called you pretty."

I snorted, but couldn't feel anything. I glanced at the statue outside of the kitchen, the look of fear frozen on his face.

"Sorry about that," I sighed.

"It's okay. He's not Diego or Eric. It would be a problem if you killed either of them, since they do a lot for me."

"Noted," I mumbled.

"You know what I hate?" Percy whispered, drawing back to look at me.

"What?" I asked.

"I hate that we could have had this all along," she said.

"Had what?"

"This. Us. That we could have been a monster and a demigod in love without hiding. That we could have just done what we wanted. Instead, we let it tear us apart because we were worried about what the others would think. But Cerberus and Ashley, Ian and Serena and Luca. They all did what they wanted and look at them now. Would it be so odd for us to be together? Would it be so wrong?"

Fuck. I couldn't handle the pain in her last question. "It's not that it's wrong," I whispered. "What if we lose what we have?"

The favors. The dates. The *friendship*.

"I washed up onto your island," Percy murmured. "I was supposed to end up there, anyway. The King had sent me to kill you. I was trying to save my mother and viewed it as a challenge from the gods."

"Yes," I whispered, remembering. "I wanted to kill you, especially when I realized you were the hero that took the lives of my sisters."

She winced, her eyes darkening as if that storm still raged within her. "We both did terrible things."

"We did," I agreed. "Our history is bloody. The books claim you killed me. That you used me. That we were enemies."

"Right," Percy whispered, leaning in closer. Her lips were almost touching mine. "Enemies."

"But I took you in. I helped you. I remember washing your body and thinking how I'd never seen a woman so beautiful before."

There were small moments like that in our star-crossed history. Moments that I tried to forget, even though they carried me through dark times. Percy didn't know all the things I had done. She didn't know why I was the way I was.

"Really? I remember you telling me I looked like Zeus came on a rock and brought it to life," Percy snorted, smirking.

I laughed, even as the heat ran through me, my breath hitching. "No. I've always thought you were beautiful."

"As are you."

The two of us fought, of course. Especially when the Three Fates Mafia was created. When the Fates brought monsters into the same city as demigods, it had been a battle. I'd stabbed her in the back as many times as she stabbed me, and yet the trust remained.

Still...

Was I really going to do this?

Was I going to finally give in?

I wasn't the type to give in. I was strong and independent and ruled my world.

But maybe she was right. Maybe we could do that together.

"Fine," I said. "I'll give this a chance."

Percy raised a brow. "Was that so hard?"

"Yes," I mumbled.

I wished I could shift back to my human form right now. It would be easier to touch her...

My body responded with the thought. I gasped as I felt the change, shifting back into the mortal version of myself, the one that made better decisions than the monstrous part.

"Thank the gods," Percy said. "That means you're getting better."

"The gods certainly didn't help," I mumbled, looking down at my legs. Gone was the long tail, the wings, the scales and talons and snakes.

I realized I was still completely naked.

We stared at each for a moment, and I decided I'd had enough. I leaned forward, closing the small gap between us. Our lips met in a soft kiss at first. But then it became raw and needy. Her fingers curled into my hair. She pushed me back onto the sofa, a low groan leaving us both as she pinned me down beneath her.

"Fuck," she rasped. "*Mads*."

I groaned. I loved it when she called me that. No one else called me by the name I preferred like she did.

I wrapped my legs around her hips as she kissed me. She let out a low groan and cupped my breasts. Her hands were warm, her fingertips sending tiny shocks scattering over my skin.

Fuck.

I didn't even think about what she could do with her demigod abilities.

She pulled back for a moment, letting out a low growl. "Fuck. Hold on. Time out."

"Time out?" I wheezed.

She paused for a moment, both of us panting. "I need to know your safeword and limits and what you like."

"Do you have any toys—"

"I have everything we could possibly need."

I smirked. "I mean we don't need them, but it would be fun..."

She sat up, looking down at me with a glint of amusement. "Do you want me to fuck you, Madeline?"

"Yes," I said. "Do you want to fuck me, Percy?"

"Yes. More than you know. What do you like?"

Normally, I'd be the one asking questions. But it felt different with her.

I wanted to be good for her.

"I like pain. I love spanking, hair pulling, rough body impact, blindfolds, humiliation, degradation, CNC...but all of those are things I've rarely let someone do to me. I don't trust anyone, and I have to trust them for that. I'm interested in your *electrical* abilities. And I'm interested in submitting to you."

"Good." She leaned down, stealing another kiss before whispering in my ear. "I'm interested in everything you are. The only thing I'll add is that I enjoy being called daddy."

"Daddy," I said. I raised a brow. "Really?"

"Yes. I'm going to go get a strap-on, and then I'm going to bend you over and fuck you like no one else ever has. Okay?"

"Please, *daddy*."

Her eyes flickered with electricity. She smiled as she slid off me and disappeared from the living room.

My heart beat faster as I waited, my pussy already wet.

She came back with a strap on and a riding crop. She stopped in front of me, regarding me with a gentle gaze.

"Are you sure, Madeline? Is your wound okay? Do you feel okay?"

"Yes," I whispered. "I want you. I want this. And right now, it's as if nothing happened." Which was the truth. The pain had faded, my body replenished with energy.

I sat up, my eyes widening as she tipped my chin with the end of the crop, making me look up at her.

"What's your safe word, kitten?"

Kitten. A shiver of excitement ran through me. Kink, BDSM, sex—none of it was new to me, and yet...with her... "Red," I whispered.

"Do you want pleasure and pain or just pleasure?"

"Both," I said. "I need both. I need to be punished."

"Do you? For what?"

"For turning your guard to stone."

"Oh," she whispered. "I won't punish you for turning a man to stone, kitten. But I will punish you for telling me you hate me."

Her words made my eyes widen. "I didn't mean that when I said it. I don't hate you."

She only smirked. "Are you taking me as a monster or mortal?"

"Mortal," I whispered.

"Then spread your legs, sweetheart. We have centuries of time to make up for."

My breath left me as I did as she said, parting my thighs for her. She knelt down again, but it wasn't an act of submission. Not with the way she was looking at me right now.

I leaned back on the couch, thighs parted, nipples hard as she pressed her lips against my core. I groaned as she dragged her tongue over my clit, pleasure working through me.

Percy groaned, driving her tongue inside me. I cried out, reaching down to bury my fingers in her silver hair, holding her perfect mouth to my pussy.

She moaned as she ate me out, her tongue working its magic. I sighed as pleasure spread through me, my eyes fluttering closed as I got closer and closer to the edge.

And then she pulled back.

"*Daddy,*" I groaned.

"Earn it, kitten," she teased. "Get up and bend over the armrest of the couch."

Chapter 8

Count

M adeline

My heart hammered in my chest. I needed more. That little taste wasn't enough.

She moved back, giving me space.

I did as she asked, standing and going around to bend over the armrest. I planted my hands on the cushion, sucking in a breath as she rose and came around.

Anticipation rolled through me. Anticipation and need. I couldn't help the way I was already feeling, the way my body reacted to her. Knowing that she was going to take me.

Percy unbuckled her belt, the sound of it making my pussy pulse. Part of me hoped she would spank me with it, craving fresh pain.

"It's been so long since I've been with someone," she said softly, her voice husky. "I can't wait to touch you."

It hadn't been long for me. I took many lovers, although none of them had ever left me satisfied. None of them were her.

How long had this secret yearning gone on?

It was impossible to say. Perhaps since I first met her.

"I've dreamed about fucking you," I whispered.

I felt like I'd just confessed my greatest secret. That yes, I had wanted her. That sometimes, in the middle of the night, I would wake up and have to make myself come because I'd dreamed about her fucking me.

Her pants fell to the floor, followed by her shirt. She wore all black, which was typical, and a cherry red thong underneath.

Fuck, that's hot.

I swallowed hard as I looked over my shoulder at her, watching as she pulled the thong free.

She grabbed the harness and fit it around her hips, the cock the perfect size for me. She winked as she spread lube over it and then stepped closer, her fingers working some into me.

I moaned, helpless, and bent over for her.

This was what I'd wanted, even if I'd never been able to admit it. To be with he freely.

The history books said we were enemies, but they had it all wrong. It had never been me against her; it had always been us against the world.

Percy was the only person in my life that ever stayed.

"Good girl," she purred. "I can feel how ready you are for my cock, kitten. I can't wait to fuck you."

All I could do was moan helplessly. She let out a low, sultry laugh—and then I flinched as I felt the soft leather of the riding crop dragging down my spine.

The anticipation was enough to drive me insane.

"How are you feeling?" she asked, checking in.

"Good. I need more. You're driving me crazy."

She ran it up and down my spine, teasing me. All while the

head of the harnessed cock pressed against my pussy. Just teasing me.

"How many people have you been with since you last dreamed of me, kitten?"

"It doesn't matter," I rasped. "Fuck. I shouldn't have told you that."

I felt the flame of embarrassment.

"But you did. And I'm glad that you did."

I swallowed hard, my thoughts a haze. I couldn't think in this position, when all I wanted was for her to bury herself into me all the way to the base.

"Count for me, kitten. Out loud."

Fuck. I closed my eyes. How many had it been? The last dream had been a couple of months ago. One that had left me wanting to hate her because of how damn good she'd been...

"One."

The riding crop popped against my skin, the pain flaring and making me gasp.

"Two," I gritted out.

She smacked me again, the sting of it making me moan. I pushed back onto the cock, but she growled, her free hand gripping my hip.

"I don't think so," she said. "Not until I let you. When I want this cock in your dripping cunt, I'll put it there. Do you understand?"

"Yes, daddy," I whimpered.

"Keep counting."

"Three." *Thwap.* "Four." *Thwap.* "Five." *Thwap.*

She alternated between my shoulders, my skin flaring with heat as she slapped me with the crop.

Six. Seven. Eight. Nine. Ten.

On the tenth, I cried out, the pain growing sharper.

"Are there more?"

"Yes," I whimpered. Tears filled my eyes, but I craved this. There was relief in the pain, an interruption to the numbness I often felt.

"You've been such a slut, haven't you? Dreaming about the demigod you claim to hate."

"I don't hate you," I whimpered. "I don't. I swear I don't. I've wanted you."

"Well, I'm here now. Spread your legs wide and push your ass out."

I did as she said, and for a moment, the head of the cock pushed inside of me. It was enough to send a jolt of pure pleasure through me, but then she pulled back.

"Fuck," I gasped.

"Keep counting for me."

"I need you inside me," I begged. "Please. There have been so many. So fucking many. And none of them have mattered, Percy. I've always needed you."

"I said *keep counting*," she commanded again.

Fuck. I'd asked for punishment and I should have known that's what I would get.

And yet my safeword didn't come to my lips.

I craved this. I longed for her to turn me into a whiny little slut that was begging for her cock.

"Eleven," I whispered.

The crop came down on my ass and I moaned, the sting sharp and sudden.

"Twelve."

She hit the other cheek.

"Thirteen."

This time, the crop smacked my pussy, and I cried out, my legs buckling. Percy waited until I regained composure.

"If you do that again, then you will not get to come."

"Yes, sir," I said. "Yes, daddy. Fourteen."

She hit my pussy again, the sting almost making me come. It was unexplainable how something like that could make me react this way, but the pleasure that hit me with the pain at the same time was euphoric.

"Your pussy is so wet," she said. "You're dripping just for me, aren't you?"

"Yes," I whined. "I need you in me."

"We'll get to twenty. How about that?"

I nodded, straightening my legs and bracing myself.

"Fifteen."

I expected it to hit my pussy again, but she slapped my ass instead. I sucked in a breath.

"Sixteen."

The crop dropped to the floor, and I felt her palm come down on my ass cheek. I gasped as she spanked me, her hand leaving a stamp of heat as she lifted it away.

I gritted my teeth, feeling my fangs sharpen. "Seventeen."

She spanked the same spot harder. I cried out, the pain intensifying.

"Eighteen." Again. "Nineteen." Again. She adjusted herself, and I gasped as I felt the head of her cock against my pussy. "*Twenty.*"

She thrust inside of me and I cried out louder than any of the other times. My body needed to be filled, and an orgasm crashed into me as she held me to her, her hands gripping my hips as I came.

"So soon," she whispered, waiting until I had finished. The aftershocks ran through me, my knees weakening.

"More," I gasped.

She only laughed, a low and wicked sound that echoed around me as she pumped in and out. The two of us moaned together as she fucked me, her movements quick-ening as she held onto me. Over and over, she thrust into me, making my entire body quiver as pleasure built up all over again.

"I'm going to come," I groaned.

"Can you, kitten?" she taunted. "*Can* you come for me again?"

"Can I?" I echoed, panting as she fucked me harder.

"Have you earned it?"

"Yes," I groaned. "I think so."

"Then come for me."

I gasped, her words reverberating through me, the command sending a shock wave through my body. I came again, crying out as my cunt squeezed her, my body draped over the couch as my muscles tensed and then loosened.

She pulled out of me with a groan and grabbed my hair, pushing me to the floor. I turned, kneeling in front of her, the cock glistening with my come.

"Take it off and make me come," she rasped.

I unhooked it quickly, the harness falling to the floor. I gripped her left calf and lifted her leg, draping her thigh over my shoulder.

I buried my face in her pussy, the taste of her making me moan. My head spun, my heart beating so loud I could hear the rush in my ears. I sucked on her clit, drawing out a soft cry from her.

I slipped two fingers inside of her, stroking her as I swirled my tongue. She gripped my hair, moaning as I edged her further, her breaths quickening.

The need to feel her coming on my face drove me, and I worked until she finally cried out, her pussy clenching around my fingers. Her head fell back, her muscles tense as she kept coming.

I pulled back, drawing my fingers from her and licking them clean.

She looked down at me, arching a brow as she panted. "Fuck. You're better than I ever dreamed."

"How many for you then?" I whispered. "How many have you been with?"

"No one in a long time, Mads," she said.

Fuck. I swallowed hard, closing my eyes as she leaned down and kissed my forehead.

"Come to the couch," she murmured.

The two of us fell into the cushions, curling up together. Her arm slipped around my shoulder, pulling me close. We were silent for a while, basking in the after orgasm glow.

Fuck.

That was better than any dream I'd ever had about her.

"How do you feel?" she asked.

"You already know," I chuckled.

Normally, I'd be sending my lover away now. I'd be slamming the door on their ass. Ordering a glass of wine and taking a long hot bath.

Normally, I'd be back to my loneliness.

But not this time.

I suddenly felt fear grip me. A fear of losing her, of losing this, of losing what we had just found.

"I don't want to tell the others," I whispered.

She stiffened against me. "We don't have to keep this secret."

"I know. But I want to wait. At least until we find the bull and end this mess with Orpheus. He'll want that blade, but I don't think he should have it."

"It's his blade, Mads."

"Yes, and look what it did. He's not a good person."

"I know he's not."

"Then you know I'm right."

She sighed heavily, relaxing again. "Can we forget about our jobs? I don't want to think about any of them right now. Nor do I want to think about the gods or the fates."

"Fine," I mumbled, relaxing. "What do we do now?"

"Watch a show, eat dinner, rest, and forget that you're a monster and I'm a demigod."

CHAPTER 9

HUNT

M adeline

I walked down Athens Avenue, disregarding the looks I got from strangers as I pushed through the front doors of my apartment building. This one was closest to the museum, the penthouse at the very top belonging to me.

It had been two days since I'd gone to Percy's. Two days of putting off my responsibilities and pretending that I didn't have to do anything else. She'd been gone through the day doing whatever she did, but then she'd come home at night.

It was almost normal. A normal life, one where we didn't have to worry about what others thought or about running two businesses. This morning I finally answered Ella's panicked texts and confused emails, and pulled myself back to reality.

I had a Minoan Bull to find.

I'd already put out feelers to a couple of informants. One of them was an assassin that many of us monsters hired when we wanted something done fast without getting our claws dirty.

Ella waited in the lobby. I would have shielded my eyes if I weren't already wearing sunglasses. She was wearing a vivid pink miniskirt and blazer, paired with nude heels and jewelry. Her eyes brightened when she saw me. It reminded me of someone I used to know, although I couldn't quite remember who.

"I was worried about you!"

"I don't see why." I waved my hand at her, irritated. Everyone was so worried about me suddenly. It pissed me off. "I was perfectly fine."

"There was a lot of blood and then you disappeared," she said quickly, following me to the elevator. "The whole city is talking about it. Especially art buyers."

She hit the button and then slid the keycard through the reader that gave us access to the very top. I let out a soft sigh. I enjoyed being at Percy's home, but it was nice to come back to a little more luxury. Her bath was not as big as mine, neither was her closet. She didn't have the clothing brands I preferred or the skincare products I used...Yet.

The thought of moving in with her made me want to melt and scream at the same time. Things were moving quickly, but neither one of us wanted anything to slow down.

"You didn't even call," Ella sniffed, clearly offended.

"You're not my keeper, Ella. You're my assistant. Now, tell me what I missed."

She sighed dramatically. "Fine." She filled me in on mundane things. My show sold out, the councilman's sudden disappearance had upset some of the mortal leaders, and I had several packages that had arrived.

"One of them is unmarked," she said. "You've always told me to never open unmarked mail, so I didn't."

"Great," I muttered. "Is it in the apartment?"

"Yeah," she said. "I left it on the counter Saturday night."

"Good," I said as the doors slid open.

We stepped into my apartment, and my eyes widened. Ella gasped, the color draining from her face.

Everything was ruined.

All of my furniture had been torn into. Someone had ripped all of my priceless paintings and broken the frames, statues smashed, glass shattered over the polished marble floors. They smeared the walls red, the scent of blood heavy.

Rage coiled through me. Someone had the audacity to fucking do this.

I would slaughter them for it.

"Ella," I said, keeping my voice even. "I need you to leave."

"What? This is horrible, this is—"

"Ella. I work alone with things like this. I need you to leave so I can keep you safe."

I ignored her gaze, ignored her protests. I turned and snapped my fingers, silencing her. I pointed to the elevator. "Go fetch me an iced latte from that coffee shop from the other side of Moirai. The one you read your monster porn novellas at."

"I can help—"

"If you say one more word, I will get a new assistant."

She clamped her mouth shut, tears in her eyes as she stepped inside and hit the button. The doors slid closed, taking her away.

I let out a slow breath and turned back around. I knew my words had hurt her, but I couldn't risk her being harmed. I'd come to care for my assistant over the last two months.

I stripped off the clothes I wore so that they wouldn't shred when I changed. I set down my bag, letting my body shift into that of a monster. My wings burst free, my auburn waves turning into writhing golden snakes. I ripped my sunglasses off, breathing in the unknown scents.

Someone had come here.

Someone had invaded my space.

And someone had been killed here.

I moved from the entry to the living room and stopped. At the center, tied to a very expensive and now destroyed designer chair, was a dead man. One that I didn't quite recognize.

"Hades, that smell," I hissed, feeling a wave of nausea.

Death wasn't new to me, but having someone rotting in my apartment certainly was. In all of my time, I could count on my perfectly manicured fingers how many bastards had the audacity to break into my home.

Percy was one of them.

What was happening? Why would someone do this?

I moved closer, studying the face. He'd been here for at least a couple days based on the scent and the bloody foam dripping from his mouth and nostrils. His body was bloated, sending another wave of disgust through me.

"For fuck's sake," I growled.

He looked familiar. It was hard to tell exactly who he was, but he was *someone*.

I slid through the wreckage that was my living room, leaving him there. There was a hall that led to the bedroom. The Greek-style busts, previously behind glass, were now shattered. Claw marks dragged down the wall, leaving a long scrape all the way to my door.

They looked like harpy claws.

I knew three harpies, and not a single one would dare cross me. So who the fuck was it?

I scowled, feeling the grooves in the drywall and paint. I let out a breath and continued bracing myself as I pushed the bedroom door open.

It creaked as my bedroom was revealed. Like the rest of the apartment, it was completely destroyed. The mattress was cut open, as were all of my pillows and velvet chair. All of the priceless art that I had collected was demolished. Statues busted, all of my clothing shredded.

Money had stopped meaning something to me in the last hundred years, but *this* still pissed me off. Some of my belongings were priceless.

This was a violation. It was personal. Whoever had done this *hated* me. The venom clung to the air, a blanket of rage and desperation.

They were trying to find something.

Did they think I had the knife? Could this have been Orpheus searching for his cursed blade? Orpheus didn't have claws, though.

Neither did the Minoan Bull.

The claws belonged to some sort of monster. Harpy or manticore...

Two monsters had come for me, then.

Mentally, I ran through all the deals I'd made in the last one hundred years. Was there something I had done? Someone I had missed? This sort of attack wasn't random.

I expected to be hunted by demigods. I expected to be hunted by men. But to be hunted by other monsters?

That, I didn't expect.

I thought about my counterparts. Cerberus, the Colchian Dragon, the Hydras, the Chimera twins. All of them had claws, but none of them would have done this.

Even when our side fought, there was still a code. Hence why the Hydras had saved my life. Despite the tension between us, we both knew I would have done the same to help them. I would have bitched about it and would have thrown them out the moment I could, but I would help.

For centuries it had been monsters fighting demigods. The gods themselves had created heroes to mock their demented children, to slowly kill us off. Zeus allowed his mortals to hate us, fear us.

Percy was the only demigod that I had ever tolerated, until recently. The new blood was decent. Naïve, nauseating with their love for my monster counterparts, but still decent.

I had wondered what the Fates were doing ever since Cerberus had found their demigod mate. I recognized beginnings and endings. This was a new era in the making.

I sighed and left the bedroom, slithering back to the front door. I grabbed my phone from my purse and called Percy.

"Hey, kitten."

Her voice nearly made my brain short circuit. My brows shot up, and it took a full two seconds for me to speak. "Percy," I hissed. "We have a problem. Well, I have a problem. I will be late for dinner."

"What happened?"

"Someone broke into my apartment and killed a mortal man. And destroyed everything."

"I'll be right there."

"No, I don't need your help—" Percy hung up before I could continue. I glared at my phone for a moment and then exhaled slowly.

What did I expect? Before, Percy might have shown concern, but she would have let me be. She might have even done me one of our infamous favors. Now, it was different.

For years, our relationship had been a dance. She'd take one step forward, I'd take one back, constantly avoiding the truth at the center of us.

It had been easier that way.

I drew in a steady breath, thinking about the past. About the walls of hate I'd built around myself because that had been better than ever letting her see me for me.

Now, she was determined to protect me from the gods and everyone else. Something inside me had shattered.

I didn't know what to do with myself.

Unlike the other Three Fates Mafia members, I didn't have a gang of hooligans that did my bidding. I had my portion of the city, which I ran excellently, and I had my assistant, Ella. Ella helped me schedule different things—lovers that volunteered their lives to me and others that didn't but still ended up in my gallery, as well as all of my shows. That gave me time to run my studio a few blocks from here. Anytime I accidentally turned someone to stone, I made sure that they weren't recognizable by the public. This often involved me breaking off their nose or cock or arm. It was cathartic.

Mortals like to jump through hoops to make things make sense. It was easier to believe I'd simply carved a likeness of their missing friend instead of seeing the truth that I was an ancient monster.

Everything else—the killing, the deals, the blood on my hands—all of it was done by me and me alone. I didn't need to do what the other mafia leaders did.

I was smart about how I ran my side of things.

But now there was a bloated corpse rotting on one of my designer chairs. All of my material possessions had been destroyed, and a bull-headed monster had almost killed me.

The past week had really been shitty.

Except for when I was with *her*.

The elevator rang, the doors sliding open. Percy stepped out, startling me. She was dressed in tailored black pants, loafers, and a blazer over a silk T-shirt.

"Were you at a meeting?" I asked.

"I was," she said. "Training a few new men with Eric. Doesn't matter."

"You have to have a key to get up here," I said, scowling at her. "You don't have a key to my apartment."

"I have one," Percy said dismissively, raising a silver brow.

My stomach did a slow somersault as she stepped past me, planting a kiss on my scaled cheek before going to the living room. I followed her and then winced as her spine stiffened.

"Fuck," she rasped. Her curses slipped into Greek, the old language making my shoulders tense.

Her hands curled into fists, a slight tremble visible.

"Percy," I whispered, stepping closer. I placed my hand on her arm, feeling the anger.

Her eyes were a searing blue, tears wetting them.

"Who is he?" I asked. "I couldn't tell..."

"Diego," she whispered. "It's Diego." She blew out a long breath, her shoulders sinking. "Gods damn it all. He was supposed to be on vacation. Something must have happened."

"I'm so sorry," I said. "I know your mortals mean something to you."

"Not all of them. But he and Eric, they have been good. He was a good man. It's hard to find them. Fuck. How the fuck did this happen?"

I didn't know. I stared at him, thinking through everyone that had a key to my place. Ella was loyal to me. They must have found another way.

If they brought Diego here, that meant that they wanted to hurt Percy, too.

And the fact that they had killed him in my place...

It was as if they were after us both. I didn't like that.

"That chair cost like four thousand dollars," I sighed.

Percy snorted despite the sadness that emanated from her. "For a chair, Mads?"

All I wanted to do was make her smile. I rolled my eyes, giving her a playful shoulder bump. "Your point? It's the little things when you've been alive for this long."

Percy nodded. She took another steadying breath and stepped closer to the body. "I have to forget I know him for now. I will grieve later. This is disturbing," she murmured. She knelt down in front of him and frowned, lifting her hand. "Do you have any gloves?"

"Oh gods," I said. "Are you going to touch him?"

"Yes. Preferably with gloves."

"Disgusting. Hold on," I grumbled.

I went to the bathroom in the bedroom, wincing at the continued destruction. I grabbed a box of gloves from the top drawer and went back to Percy, handing it to her.

She pulled out a pair and put them on, humming to herself. "There's something inside of him. If you're squeamish, then you should look away."

I opened my mouth to argue that I had seen plenty of bodies in my life, but then she stuck her fingers into a wound and it *squelched.*

"For fuck's sake," I snarled, turning around. I crossed my arms, holding my breath as the scents in the room became stronger. I pulled my wings in tight, my shoulders stiffening.

"These wounds are from a knife," Percy said. "He's been stabbed multiple times. There's a lot of infection around each wound, that is...weird. Not normal, given that he's dead. I wonder if it was *the* knife. And...*what the fuck?*"

"What?" I asked. "I'm not turning around."

"It's a drachma. Each knife wound has some shoved into it."

"For Charon?" I asked, scowling.

"We both know the coin has no value to him," Percy sighed. "You don't know how this happened? Why he might be here?"

"I don't," I confirmed, still not turning around. "I've been with you, Percy."

"I know." I heard her take the gloves off. "Let's look through the entire apartment. We will figure out who did this. You said they have to have used a key. Who else has a key?"

"Me, Ella, and apparently you. How did you get one?"

Percy ignored my question. "Would they have a key in the office downstairs?"

"Yes, I'm sure. Percy, how did you get a key?"

She sighed. "I stole it a while back and made a copy."

"What? When?"

"Like eight months ago when we went to that opera. You thought you left your key there."

"You bitch," I mumbled. "How do I know it wasn't you that did this?"

I felt her step up behind me, her hand gripping several snakes. I gasped, and they hissed as she pulled my head back, her lips close to the curve up my neck.

"You know I would never hurt you like this," she whispered, her voice dark. It felt like a threat, one that made my nipples harden. "And why would I kill my own man? He was valuable to me."

I swallowed hard.

"I took the key in case I needed to help you someday. Like today," she said, her voice still cold. "It could have been you that was attacked here. What if I needed to save you? You can have a key to my house in exchange."

A shiver worked through me. *Now* was not the time to be turned on by her. "I'll take a key," I said. "I'm sorry about Diego."

I turned around, only to be tugged against her. She tipped my chin up, her eyes blazing.

"You just touched a dead body," I protested, faking a gag.

"I was wearing gloves," she said. Her lips slowly tugged into a smile, but it was edged with vehemence. With hurt.

I didn't like to see her hurt.

"I'll find who did this and I will kill them the 9th century way."

"I can fight my own battles," I whispered.

"I know you can. I've never doubted you for a moment," she said, releasing me. "But this isn't just your battle. This is personal to me. Why would they kill one of my men in *your* home?"

"If I knew, then I wouldn't just be standing here."

She took a step back and pulled her phone out, already making calls. It dawned on me that I'd sent Ella on an errand, so while Percy made arrangements, I sent my assistant a text to take the day off. She could enjoy the latte for me.

Within thirty minutes, I was redressed as Madeline—sunglasses, human legs, and all—and my apartment was swarming with her men. The body was gone, and Eric had combed the whole place over.

They'd found nothing I hadn't found. The claw marks definitely belonged to a harpy. Diego's blood splattered the walls and the floor in the kitchen. Aside from that, there wasn't much else. It wasn't like we had a database with fingerprints for monsters or their DNA to identify them.

We were shit out of luck.

"Sorry, Mistress," Eric said, wincing at Percy. "I've looked through everything. Diego..."

"Do you know his family?" Percy asked. "He was supposed to be on vacation."

"I can reach out to them. We will figure it out," Eric said, his voice strained. "I will not rest until I find out who hurt him."

"I promise you I will avenge him, Eric," Percy said. "I will make them suffer."

He nodded, giving her a look that could only be described as adoration. I could see why they respected her as much as they did.

She meant every word she said. She would find who killed Diego and she would make them wish they'd never crossed her. It was that type of power that I enjoyed watching her wield.

Over the years, the two of us had claimed our power. Our strength. It made us ruthless bitches, but that was the price we paid in a world of men.

That someone had felt comfortable enough to do this in my apartment meant that I'd been slacking.

"I don't know if I want a drink or to go on a bloody rampage."

"Both," Percy said, glancing over at me.

My gaze swept around my destroyed apartment again. "I think a drink first."

Percy dismissed Eric and then came to me. "I'll join you. Do you want to bring anything with you? I can have it sent to my place."

"To your place? I have another house."

"Yes, and we probably need to see if it's been destroyed too."

I felt a flicker of sadness. What if they'd destroyed everything there, too?

"Let's go get a drink at one of my clubs. Then we'll go to your house. If there's anything wrong there, then we'll figure it out. I promise we will figure this out," Percy said.

"Someone is hunting me," I whispered, my voice trembling with anger. "Someone came into my space and did this believing there wouldn't be consequences."

She cupped my face, making me look at her. "And we will find them. There will be plenty of consequences. They won't attack us when we're together."

"How do you know?"

"Who would dare? Not even the other members of the mafia would be so stupid."

True.

I drew in a steadying breath. There was something that I needed to say. "Hey, Percy..."

"Yes?"

"I changed my mind about keeping us a secret. I don't care if they know. I don't care if the whole world knows."

She smiled. It was a smile that lit up the entire room, shedding warmth on the situation we were in. "Okay, Madeline."

I cleared my throat and straightened my back. "Anyway. Let's go to one of your clubs."

Percy nodded and looped her arm in mine, leading me to the elevator. "You'd be surprised what you can find in that sort of atmosphere. We'll go to the one on this block. Perhaps a mortal saw Diego."

"I doubt it," I said. "Their memories are faulty."

She gave me a soft chuckle. "You never know, Mads. You never know."

CHAPTER 10

SEX ROOM

P ercy

Andromeda was a two-story club that was only a block from Madeline's high-rise apartment. A couple of streets over was the Cerberus penthouse, and near to there, the Colchian's. Despite the way we split the city up, downtown Moirai was covered with all our businesses.

We stepped through the red front door. Stickers and graffiti covered the surrounding frame. I breathed in the scent of smoke, liquor, and sex.

Madeline glanced back at me, my visage a reflection in her sunglasses. We smiled at each other. I reached down and slipped my hand into hers.

It was a small touch, but it meant more than I had words for. I was openly holding her hand in public.

She'd told me we didn't have to be a secret, put part of me expected her to still pull her friend free.

Instead, her grip tightened in mine.

My heart pounded in my chest. I could feel the lustful gaze of onlookers. Everyone wanted her, but they'd never have her. I'd forgotten the magnetism Madeline had in a crowd. I tugged her close to me, the two of us pushing through the mortals that danced with each other.

I was doing my best to bury the pain I felt. Someone had captured Diego and had stabbed him to death. Someone that held the belief that Charon required a coin.

They killed him brutally and then gave him a gift for the afterlife. None of this made sense.

The club lights flashed different shades of blue. Ahead of us, a set of stairs lead to a balcony with a polished marble high-top bar. I kept my businesses clean and modern, but just slutty enough to attract the right crowd.

Jack, the bartender, recognized me immediately and began pouring my regular. I gave him a knowing nod as I slid onto the leather barstool. Madeline sat on the one next to me, her glasses reflecting the lights. Her hand slid over my thigh under the bar, sending a wave of heat through me.

Madeline snorted, gesturing at the neon pink sign on the wall. "I don't know if she would like a club named after her."

"Well, she's dead," I said simply.

She laughed, the sultry sound going straight to my pussy. I loved it when she laughed. "Fucking hell. Remind me to never piss you off."

I shrugged. "It's not that she pissed me off."

"She did. I remember hearing about it."

"Simply rumors."

"Oh sure. Is that why almost every establishment you've ever owned has had this name? You know she would hate that. She was a prudish cunt."

I gave her a flat look, but stopped denying it. Andromeda

had pissed me off. And yes, this was a way to spite her. She would have fainted if she knew I had named a club after her.

"Here's you regular, Mistress," Jack said, sliding me a Negroni neat. His attention turned fully to Mads, his eyes widening with adoration. "What can I get for you, madam?"

"Peachy keen, please."

"Of course. Give me just a moment."

I wanted to roll my eyes at him. Instead, I turned on the barstool and looked out over the club. I studied the crowd, looking for anyone of interest. Anyone that stood out. Mortals danced with each other, the crowd moving in sync with the music. All of them blended together, nothing of interest drawing my attention.

Within a few moments, Jack brought us Madeline's drink. She took it, immediately picking up the skewered peach slice.

"Thanks." She bit into it, her gaze meeting mine.

Now she would taste like peaches. My mouth watered and I looked away.

I would remember that later. I cleared my throat and spoke. "Jack. Have you heard anything strange? Or seen anyone that felt off? You have a good eye for bizarre things. That's why I hired you."

Jack let out a hum and leaned against the bar, thinking. He had a short black beard and tattoos crawling over his forearm and neck. His eyes lit up as he remembered something.

"There was someone in here bragging about their boss giving them a raise. It was rather obnoxious. You would have thought they'd won the lotto. Do you have something specific you're looking for? I can keep my ear to the ground."

"Someone broke into my apartment and destroyed everything," Madeline hissed, focusing on him. "And someone killed Diego. Do you know Diego, bar man?"

I watched his face become slack, his pupils expanding as he

looked at her. Even with the glasses on, her influence on mortals was strong.

She leaned forward, giving him a sensuous smile. "What do you know, sugar? Someone like you knows a lot. That's why she hired you, huh?"

He flushed, his hands trembling. I raised a brow and took a sip of my drink, enjoying her show a little too much.

"Diego was here. He looked frightened," Jack said. "I asked him if he was okay and he told me to fuck off. He's not normally like that."

He wasn't. Diego was always calm and collected, even when killing. "Was he hiding from someone? Running?"

"No," Jack said. "I don't know."

"Honey, we need to know more. Search that big brain for more answers."

He frowned, clearly thinking hard.

"I can check footage," I said, glancing at Madeline.

"He has more," she said.

"I..I...there was this man."

"Describe him," she purred, stirring her drink with the tip of her finger. She brought it to her lips, sucking it.

Fuck.

I narrowed my eyes at her, feeling a streak of possessiveness. I could feel others watching us.

"He wore a suit and tie. He had someone else with him, a brother."

Alarm bells went off in my head. "Were they twins, Jack?"

He blinked a couple times as he registered my question, having forgotten I even existed. "Yes, I think so. It's hard to know. They looked different, but their mannerisms were similar. They asked me a question, but I don't...I don't remember anything."

They'd probably drugged him. "When was this?" I pressed.

"Two nights ago. They were drinking. Two whiskies. They were going hunting."

"Did they have green eyes?" Madeline asked, her tone strained.

"They told me to give you this," Jack continued, his eyes wide and voice faraway.

My shoulders stiffened as he reached into his shirt pocket, pulling out a card. It was black with gold foil, the writing at the center clear.

'You're being hunted—Chimera.'

I blew out a breath and passed the card to Madeline. She let out a low growl.

I downed my Negroni and then stood. "Change of plans tonight. Let's go see the twins."

"They couldn't have called?" Madeline snarled.

"They like to play the game," I said. "You know this."

She pressed her lips together, but she knew I was right. The Chimera twins were my least favorite of all the monsters in our mafia. I would take arguing with Argos, Damon, or even Ian over one of them.

They were liars and tricksters.

"First the bull, then the dead man and destroyed apartment. I didn't think the claw marks belonged to them," Madeline said. She stood up and waved at Jack. "Go back to your work, mortal. We don't need you anymore."

Her tone seemed to break whatever spell she'd cast over him. He wandered down the bar in a daze.

I sighed, disgruntled. This wasn't how I wanted to spend the night.

"Fuck them," Madeline growled. "Hold on. We aren't going to them."

She pulled out her phone and hit a number, holding it to her ear. She held my gaze as she spoke.

"Paris," she said venomously, raising her voice over the music. "You and Ty will come to Perseus's home tomorrow for brunch. Hmm. Yes. No, I don't really care if you have a meeting. If you don't show up, then I will destroy your favorite building downtown."

"Madeline," I hissed, glancing around us. Her words earned us a couple of alarmed glances.

Her lips twisted into a cruel smile. "Brunch it is, then. I can't wait to see you both."

She hung up and crossed her arms. "There. They'll be there tomorrow. Now, I can enjoy the rest of my evening before I just take my glasses off and turn everyone to stone."

"Well," I muttered. "That's one way to do it."

She snorted. "You really think I would ever meet them on their own turf? If they are a part of this, then I want them in a place they are unfamiliar with."

"That makes sense. I probably would have thought about that if I weren't so distracted."

"Oh? And what are you distracted by, darling?"

I pulled her closer to me, our lips hovering. "What do you think, kitten?"

She sucked in a breath, her chin tilting up. I slid my palm against her cheek, pressing my forehead to hers. "Am I really driving you that crazy?"

More than she knew. I wanted her. I *craved* her.

Everything that was happening around us frustrated me. Worried me. Knowing what Clotho had said frightened me. Every moment I had with Madeline felt like it was rushing us to the end. An end I would do anything to prevent.

I would find the knife. I would kill the Fates if I had to in order to save her.

Over the last couple of days, I'd realized there was no line I wouldn't cross for her.

I would go to Tartarus and back if that meant I could hold her forever.

"Percy," she whispered. "Everyone is staring at us."

"Let them," I murmured, brushing my lips over hers. I tasted the peaches, tasted the alcohol. I wanted to drink her in, to drown myself in her. I paused, whispering in her ear. "I'm going to fuck you tonight, kitten. I'm going to make you scream. I'm going to make you beg."

We both needed the release.

Her hand curled into my shirt, gripping me hard as I kissed her again. Her lips parted, our tongues meeting in hunger. In desperation.

Tomorrow, we would deal with the aftermath of what had happened the last few days. But for tonight, she was mine. Mine and mine alone.

I let out a soft growl and broke the kiss. I gripped her hair, enjoying her gasp. "Let's get out of here."

"Okay," she whispered.

I slipped my hand into hers and led her back through the crowd. Within a few minutes, we were back in my car, Eric driving us to my home.

I'd never been so thankful for the shield between the front seat and back.

Madeline straddled my lap, grinding her pussy against me. I let out a soft groan and hiked her dress up, need gripping me. I grabbed her hips, kissing her throat as she moaned. "I want you in your monster form tonight," I huffed.

"I don't know," she whined. "I..."

"I wasn't *asking*, kitten," I growled, slipping two fingers into her panties. She was already wet for me. She gripped my shoulders, groaning as I circled her clit. "I'm taking you as I please. I have plans in mind. You have your safeword if you want me to stop."

"Fuck," she gasped. Her hips thrust against my hand, her moans growing louder. "I hope you know you're the only person in the world I will submit to."

"I know," I said. "And I cherish that trust, Madeline, I really do."

Thirty minutes later, I was pushing her through my front door. I stripped her dress off and kicked the door shut behind us, reaching back to lock it.

"I want to touch you," she said.

"Take off my clothes," I commanded.

Her touch softened, her smile sensuous. She reached up and cupped my face, stroking my cheek before she slid her hands down to my jacket.

My blood felt like it was on fire. I needed more. I needed her.

She stripped my clothes off, tossing them to the side until we were both naked. I lifted her, pulling her legs around my waist as I carried her up the staircase to a new room in the house.

I knew what I needed right now. What we both needed.

"What room is this?" she asked.

I opened the door and took her to a chair, one that was shaped like a horizontal S. I pinned her there, our lips almost touching.

"This is a sex room." She smiled, raising a brow.

"Turn," I whispered.

Her smile faded, her eyes narrowing. "You'll like me better this way," she said.

"Turn," I demanded. "I know that your mortal form takes energy to maintain, and I want you to let go right now. Let go of everything, Mads."

"Does the hero have a monster kink?" she teased.

"I have a Madeline kink."

She stared at me for a moment, and then sucked in a slow breath. "You're absurd."

"Were you lying to me when you told me the things you like?" My question was firm. It was harsh. And I needed it to be.

Her eyes widened. "No. None of that was a lie."

"Then I want you to turn for me. As I asked. Without protest. Because that's what I want. And you want to please me."

"I do," she said, her voice softening. "Fine. I'll do it for you."

I stood and watched as she changed before my eyes. Madeline was beautiful no matter what form she was in. But, there was a part of me that wanted to push her. To remind her she could be just as loved and admired in this form as her other.

That she didn't need to hide from me.

Hell, that she *couldn't* hide from me.

Her tail wrapped around the room, the scales glittering gold and green. Wings stretched behind her, her arms lifted above her head. Her nipples were hard, diamond shaped pupils expanding as she watched me.

"Good girl," I whispered. "You're beautiful like this."

"Stop," she whispered.

"No," I said. "You're stunning. I cherish you, kitten. Every part of you. I want you to touch yourself for me while I pick out a couple of things."

"Yes, *daddy*."

Fuck. I watched as she slid her hand down her body, parting the slit below her hips. My pussy pulsed as I watched. It took every ounce of control to turn and walk to the armoire I kept.

She was right about one thing. This *was* a sex room. This was where I would do all sorts of depraved, kinky, delicious things. I kept many objects here, objects for pleasure and for pain. There was a Saint Andrew's Cross in the corner, one that I would bind her to later. A wooden spanking bench sat next to it, leather padding on the base to kneel on. The S chaise was at the center. Then there was my armoire of toys.

Pain and pleasure. Two of my favorite things.

I opened the armoire, looking at all the items I kept. The paddles, the floggers, the riding crops, rope, and other sex toys. I had collected many items, all of which I enjoyed using. I enjoyed the feel of rope against my palms as I tied up my willing subject, or the feel of the paddle on their ass as I punished them. Savored the sounds they made, and the feeling of being in control.

There was a sadistic and cruel part of me that hungered to cause pain. I was not a bad person, despite my past struggles with that notion. I never wished to actually harm someone I cared about, but hurting them? That brought me immense joy.

I had lived a long time and was a mafia boss. I had to be harsh, mean, and controlling. I did everything I could to live. To fulfill the destiny the Fates set out before me.

There was the Three Fates Mafia Percy, and then there was the bedroom Percy.

Here, I could still give in to those tendencies, but it felt different. The person on the receiving end *wanted* what I did to them.

Just like she wanted what I would give to her tonight.

I chose pink hemp rope, throwing it over my shoulders. The feel of the material was rough, adding a pleasant sensation of friction. The vibrations as the rope dragged over her scales would turn her on.

I also picked out a flogger, lube, and a vibrator wand. I was certain she could take it all for me in her monster form.

She let out a soft moan. I glanced over my shoulder, seeing

that she was still obeying so well. I chuckled as I crossed the room to her.

"Rope?" she asked.

"Yes. Have you been tied up before?"

"Once or twice. I normally do the tying."

"Hmm. Maybe I'll let you make a decorative tie for me at some point."

"Yes," she breathed out. "I'd love to. But for now..."

"I'll tie you," I said, planting a kiss on her forehead.

Two snakes hissed at me, and I ignored their love bites. Their fangs barely hurt.

One thing that I had learned about Madeline long ago was that the snakes were merely an extension of her emotions. They were not separate beings capable of independent thought. They were her, as much as her wings or tail were. The only difference was that they bit.

I knew that fucking her as a monster might break her in some ways. Her emotions would run higher. I didn't know every part of her history. I was aware there could be landmines we could hit because of that.

What the books told and what actually happened were two different things.

But I wanted to see her break.

Not because I wanted to harm her.

But because I wanted her to see what I saw. The only way that would happen was if I bulldozed the stone walls around her precious heart.

I wanted her to see the woman that had survived centuries of the patriarchy. A woman that had built her own empire. A woman that had helped other women survive the atrocities of life.

She was art.

She was sin.

She was a goddess.

And she was the altar I wanted to forever pray upon.

I loved her. I loved her so much. So how could she hate herself? How could she hate anything about herself when I loved every part of her? It offended me.

"Be a good girl for me, Mads, and put your wrists together."

CHAPTER 11

CONFESSIONS

M adeline

My nipples hardened as the rope pulled over my skin. Percy bound my wrists, drawing them over my head and securing them to a rig point she'd added to the base of this chaise.

I watched her expression as she worked. The longer I laid here, the further I felt myself falling into subspace.

She was the only person I'd ever been able to truly relax around. I trusted her more than anyone else. I knew she cared for me. I knew that she was here for me.

My muscles relaxed, the vibrations rolling through my body as she tied more of me. Every movement brought soft moans from me, little noises here and there.

I was in a cathedral.

She was worshiping me.

My breath hitched as she wrapped the ropes around my breast, tying it in a way that squeezed. It was tight enough that I could already see the blush of blood beneath my skin. It felt like she was gripping me, my nipple becoming more sensitive as she did the other.

There was nothing I could do. I was a slave to pleasure, trusting the woman the entire world claimed was my enemy.

She paused for a moment, flicking one of my nipples. I gasped as pleasure curled through me. I arched against the chaise.

She chuckled, circling it slowly. I groaned, helpless to her. "You're so sensitive," she teased.

I nodded, my breath hitching as she continued to tie a diamond shape down my body. Her fingers brushed my stomach and hips, trailing down to where my scales began.

"How long is the rope?"

"I have all the rope I could possibly need for you," she said.

I watched her, enjoying the way she concentrated. She had me enamored.

There had been so many times over the years that I had thought she was beautiful. But then, I would chastise myself for thinking so. *She's a demigod. She's the enemy.*

For the first time, I let myself think that without guilt. Without shame.

Percy was beautiful.

She leaned down, pressing her lips against my slit. I gasped, an electrical sensation rolling through me just from her touch. Every nerve ending in my body was alive, craving more. Needing more.

"Do you remember that night in Paris?" she asked, her voice sweet.

"What night? Which one?"

"1721. The night that I ran into you in the gardens. You were using magic to hide. I never asked how you did that."

"How I made myself appear like a mortal?"

"Yes," she said.

"Before the Fates gifted me a form I could always use, I would do favors for Eris. In return, she would give me a talisman with limited use. Our relationship didn't have the best ending, but it worked out since the Fates had their own plans. The pact of the gods where they *swore* they'd have no more offspring."

She smiled. "The gods are liars. We both know this."

Was that sadness or anger, or both? "Percy. You used to worship them. And love them."

"It's difficult to maintain faith in a father that thinks dust is more worthy than you."

"Surely he never said such a thing," I growled.

"He didn't have to. His absence is loud enough." She finished tying the rope and then looked up at me, the air crackling between us. "I want to focus on us, kitten. No one else in the universe matters right now."

"Okay," I said.

She smiled, and I felt everything else fall away. She leaned forward and kissed my scales. I writhed against her, not used to someone touching me this way. She was slow and deliberate, every kiss measured as she made her way up to my slit.

I let out a soft breath. "*Daddy.*"

"Good girl," she hummed. "You know I like it when you call me that."

I hissed between my teeth, my head falling back as her tongue circled my opening. She parted it, holding me there as she lapped at my clit. Pleasure rushed through me, every muscle in my body tensing as she teased me.

My back arched against the chaise as she continued. She slipped two fingers inside of me, making a *come-hither* motion with them as her tongue whirled around my clit.

I gasped, feeling another electric shock from her. It went straight to my core, almost making me come instantly.

"Fuck," I gasped. This was unlike anything I've ever done before.

She moaned against my pussy and then pulled back. "That's all for now, kitten."

"What? I need more," I groaned.

"Then earn it."

I let out another curse as she rose, her eyes darkening as she reached for a small flogger. The scent of leather turned me on. The one that she held had a woven leather handle and ended in bright blue tails.

She dragged the endings over my skin, featherlight touches from my hips to my breasts. It was soft over my skin, sending many sensations through me. I sucked in a breath as she came to my nipples, my breast squeezed from the rope that she had bound them with.

She straddled me, grinding her pussy against mine as she held my gaze. The only person in the world that could. She dragged the flogger over my skin again and then lifted it, suddenly striking one of my breasts. The sound of the leather on skin was like a clap, the strike easy but still sending a shockwave through me. Being bound this way, everything was more intense. I couldn't escape her.

She could do whatever she wanted to me.

The thought pleased me more than I imagined possible.

"Remember your safeword," she breathed.

It was clear that was the last time she would remind me.

I nodded, captivated, as she lifted the flogger and struck me again. She started a rhythm, striking each breast over and over again. I groaned as they became harder, gasping as marks slowly formed. I could see the outline of the leather tails.

I was falling deep into subspace. Everything was fading around me. I craved release, but above that, I craved to please her.

Thwack. Thwack. Thwack.

I was so fucking wet.

She rocked her hips against me, still straddling me. The movement made me feral, a desperate growl leaving me.

"Please," I groaned. "I want you to make me come."

"We're just getting started. Be patient, sweetheart."

"Patience isn't my strong suit."

"I can gag you, if you'd like."

I snapped my mouth shut, narrowing my eyes on her smirk. She struck me again, this time harder. Pain flared, followed by tail curling euphoria.

"All these marks," she huffed. "They look good on you."

I could feel how wet she was as she rocked her hips. She was driving me crazy.

She continued to flog my breasts until I had tears in my eyes, a groan leaving me. She tossed the flogger to the side and leaned down, tracing the welt lines with the tip of her tongue. I panted as I held her gaze.

The look in her eyes...*fuck.*

She circled my nipple and then bit down.

"*Fuck.*"

My heart thundered in my chest, my eyes fluttering as I gasped. She sucked and bit, teasing each one until I felt like I was going to fall apart.

I bucked my hips and writhed beneath her. My movements did nothing but put more fire in her gaze. She kissed between my breasts, and then up to the hollow of my collarbone.

"You're beautiful," she whispered. "Stunning."

"No," I whimpered.

I could handle raw sexual desire. I could handle degradation and hearing that I was a slut or whore or fuck toy. But hearing her call me beautiful, that hurt more than anything else.

"You know that you're gorgeous," she said. "I've seen you

use it to your advantage. Like tonight in the club." She went on kissing my body, moving back down to my stomach. "I want to mark every part of you as mine."

"I'm beautiful as a human."

"And as a fierce monster," she purred.

I swallowed back tears. They stung more than the flogger. "You're wrong."

"I'm not wrong," she said. Her voice was so matter of fact. "I have good taste, don't I? I have high standards."

I hesitated. She let out a low growl and gripped my chin, forcing me to look at her.

"Do I not? Have you seen the people I've chosen to be with in the past? They were always the best of the best."

"Yes," I whispered. "That doesn't mean I'm the best."

"It means that you're better than the best. You are my mate, Madeline," she whispered. "Do you have so little faith in the Fates?"

"Yes," I said, swallowing hard. "Maybe they made a mistake."

"Is what we're doing a mistake?"

No. Of course, the answer was no. For the first time in centuries, I'd let myself feel true happiness. I'd let myself be with someone that I trusted more than anyone else on this fucking planet.

"Just make me come," I rasped. "Please."

She snorted and cupped my face. *"Baby..."*

I felt everything inside me melt. Every damn wall I'd built up, the years of hurt. Tears sprang to my eyes again, and I sniffled. "You're a cunt," I whimpered.

She smirked and planted a kiss on my lips. I didn't want it to stop, my tongue meeting hers. She reached down between us as we kissed, pushing two fingers inside me.

Fuck.

She moved them, pleasure rolling through me as we kept kissing. I arched against her, pulling against the ropes, to no avail.

She broke our kiss and pulled her hand free, sliding off me.

"I swear to the gods," I gasped. "I'm going to literally combust if you don't let me come."

Percy snorted and picked up the vibrator wand, raising a brow at me. She pressed the button. "You can thank me after, in bed, kitten."

CHAPTER 12

MEMORIES

P ercy

I held the vibrator to her pussy, enjoying the way she cried out. The more I learned about her, the more ideas I had for what I wanted to do to her in the bedroom.

She gasped as pleasure rolled through her, her hips moving. I was so wet from touching her, watching her.

I loved bringing her pleasure. I loved bringing her pain. In fact, I loved everything about her.

Her cry rang through the room as she finally came for me. I kept on holding the vibrator to her even as she came.

"Fuck," she gasped. "Fuck!"

"Come again for me," I said, upping the vibration intensity.

She groaned, her muscles coiled as I edged her further. I felt a wave of immense satisfaction as she came again, her cries bringing me a euphoric sort of joy.

She relaxed beneath me. I hit the button on the vibrator,

turning it off. I leaned down, gripping her chin. She parted her lips, her tongue touching the tip of her fangs.

I held her gaze, knowing that if I were anyone else in the world, she would turn me to stone.

"You did so good for me," I murmured. "And tomorrow night I will push you further. You can turn back to human now."

She whimpered, her body already changing. I watched as she went from a beautiful monster to an equally beautiful human.

Eventually, I would show her that being a monster wasn't a bad thing. But it would take some time, and perhaps some deviousness, on my part.

I had a plan. One that would take a bit of preparation but would be worth it. Until then...

The ropes loosened around her human form. I untied her wrists, allowing her to finally, completely, relax. She let out a soft hum, still floating on cloud nine, as I unknotted all the rope. I took it slow, dragging the rope over her skin sensuously. Untying the rope was just as sacred as tying it. I appreciated the rope marks indenting her soft skin, the way she shivered with every movement I made.

I caressed her breasts, appreciating the marks there.

"How do you feel?" I asked.

"I feel so good." She looked at her breasts and blushed. "That turns me on."

"Me too," I said, smirking.

I kissed her skin gently, massaging them.

"Percy..." she moaned. "What about you? I want to make you come."

"You will, kitten," I said. I tossed the rope to the floor and then looked up at her. "There's no orgasm scoreboard, you know. Just because I make you come twice doesn't mean you have to do the same for me. Perhaps I'll take advantage of you later."

She nodded, giving me a soft smile. She parted her lips to speak and then shut them.

"What?" I asked. "Tell me what you're thinking."

"I know that you have high standards. I know you would not be with me if I did not meet those standards. But, for so long, I've been a monster in the eyes of humanity. Sometimes I struggle with loving myself because hate is so much easier. I'm working on it."

I'd never heard such vulnerability from her, and I felt honored that she would share that thought. I slid my hand into hers, our fingers intertwining. She gave it a gentle squeeze.

"I just need you to be patient with me," she whispered. "And I will work on those things."

"I've been patient this long," I said. "I would wait for you for another eternity if I needed to, Madeline."

I slipped my arms underneath her body, lifting her. She looped her arms around my neck, holding onto me as I carried her out of the room. I would clean everything else up later.

Even though we've known each other for so long, everything felt new. The emotions, our words and thoughts.

"I know that I'm asking a lot of you to be like this with me," I said softly. "But I cherish you. More than I can express in words. I want you to feel safe. I want you to know that we can be like this with each other."

"Thank you."

I kicked open the bedroom door and carried her to my bed. Even though we've been together the last few days, I'd usually been sleeping on the couch downstairs to give her space.

I laid her down on the blankets, but instead of her letting go of me, she pulled me down with her. I lifted the blankets, the two of us situating ourselves so that we were comfortable.

She pressed her forehead to mine, the two of us facing each other.

"I want to please you," she murmured.

"You do please me," I said.

"You know what I mean."

"How about this? For now, we cuddle. And then if you'd still like to make me come, wake me up in the middle of the night with your tongue on my clit. I like midnight surprises. Or whatever time it is."

She smirked, her hand sliding up to cup my cheek. "I can surprise you, then?"

"Yes," I said. "I can't think of a better way to wake up than with a gorgeous woman between my thighs."

"Deal."

"Good," I said.

Silence settled between us. My thoughts turned to the morning, to what awaited us tomorrow. Paris and Ty would be here, we would question them, and I had a feeling that they would be difficult. I appreciated that she'd forced them here, though.

"Tomorrow we will meet with the twins. And if they were part of what happened to Diego, I will start a war."

"*We* will start a war," she corrected. "We would have most of the mafia on our side. The new demigods like you, not to mention that they believe in justice. They haven't been around long enough to be corrupted yet. Cerberus and the Colchian would support us too."

"I know they would support *you*," I said. "I'm not so certain that they would support me. Ashley and Serena are good, yes. And our relationship is fine. But I still don't know them, and they don't know me very well. I am one of the older demigods, whether I like it or not. Orpheus and Theseus are crusty old bastards. And maybe I am too, even though I don't look like it."

She laughed, shaking her head. "Don't be ridiculous," she said. "You're nothing like the others. There's a reason that I have done favors for you for so long. And that I've asked you for favors as well. When I've said that I've hated demigods in the past, I didn't mean you. Perhaps at first. But we've really been through everything together, haven't we?"

"We have," I agreed.

And I couldn't help but wonder how things would've changed if we had pursued our relationship earlier on. It was something that I had always ignored, the instinct that she belonged to me.

How different would things be now if the day I washed up on her island, I had become hers?

I needed to tell her about Clotho. I knew I needed to, and yet I couldn't bring myself to speak the words. Because I was still trying to create some sort of plan to get out of the situation. A way to please the Fates that would allow me to keep my mate.

I needed to find the knife.

I could either use it to fight Clotho or barter with her. I had to find a way. Now that I knew Madeline was mine, I couldn't simply let her go.

She turned over, and I wrapped my arm around her waist. The two of us sighed, relaxing into each other. She smelled like sex and sin and pleasure. I breathed her in before closing my eyes.

My thoughts kept bouncing between the present, the past, and the future.

My eyes fluttered, sleep plunging me into a memory.

I stared out the window of the train car, watching as London went by. My body ached, a bone deep exhaustion settling over me. I had been on the frontline for the last few months, but the war was finally ending.

For the first time, humans had the power of gods. And, of course, they were using it to destroy each other.

A soft knock had me looking up at the door. I'd booked my own private cart for a reason, needing to be away from everyone.

"Percy," a soft voice said.

One I recognized.

I stood up quickly and threw open the door. Medusa, or whatever name she was using right now, stood on the other side. She smiled, lifting her glasses.

"Can I come in?"

Her hair was pulled back, her clothing that of an upper class woman. What was she doing on this train?

"Yes," I said, stepping out of the way. She slid by me, her breasts brushing against me as she did so. I swallowed hard, shutting the door.

She sat in the seat across from mine, arching a perfect brow. A table was between us, a cold and untouched cup of coffee waiting.

"What brings you here? You look...ghastly."

"What's with the fake transatlantic accent?" I asked.

She rolled her eyes as she folded her sunshades.

"Do those really help?" I asked, eyeing them.

"Yes, they do. They seem to keep me from turning people to stone. I just tell people my doctor makes me wear them. Mortals believe anything."

I felt a streak of bitterness as I leaned back into my seat. "What do you want? I'm tired and hungry. I've been trying to keep these mortals from offing themselves," I grumbled.

The last time we met, she had pissed me off. She'd used information I had from Orpheus to help another monster. It nearly cost me that connection. Orpheus was a bastard through and through, and not someone I needed as an enemy right now.

"Did you receive the letter?" she asked. Her voice was wary, her gaze piercing.

"What letter?" I asked.

She reached into her bag and pulled out a manila envelope. I felt my stomach twist as she handed it to me. There was a cracked golden seal on the front, the symbol of the Fates stamped there.

It had been years since I'd heard from the Gods or the Fates. Part of me was convinced that they had forsaken us all, and yet in my hands I had proof that they still existed.

Had they just stopped caring?

I pulled out a piece of paper, unfolding it to read the scrawled ink words.

Dear Medusa,

We have selected you to live amongst the mortals. We are forming a coalition of demigods and monsters that will work for us. You, along with four other monsters, are chosen to form half of the mafia. The other half will belong to demigods.

In exchange for your cooperation, we will give you a permanent mortal form you may shift into. You will be given wealth, power, and control over your life. No longer will you have to hide in the shadows of men.

Come to Moirai City, to the tallest building on October 1st, 12pm sharp.

—Clotho, Lachesis, Atropos

"Is this letter real?" I was doing my best not to let my hands shake.

"Yes," she said. "Although their handwriting is shit. I could barely make it out. I have been contacted by two other monsters who received the invitation."

"Who are they?" I asked.

"Cerberus and the Colchian dragon..." she trailed off. "The only demigod I know of is Hercules. I am not pleased. I need you to be chosen for this."

"Why?" I looked up at her, feeling my heart beat faster. "Why, Medusa?"

"It's still Mary at the moment," she sighed. "And what do you mean, why? They will murder the others. This is a purge."

"They wouldn't kill demigods," I snorted. "We've been around for ages."

"So have the monsters," she said. "Longer than you, in fact. And I have seen what the Fates do to us. They do not love us. They do not care. Neither do the gods. We are alone in this world, and this is a ticket to survival." She stood up, plucking the letter from my grip. "If you have to kill another in order to hold such a letter, do it. I will see you then. Call this a favor for you."

"Wait," I said. "Can you at least stay for a drink? This train has another hour."

She studied me for a moment and then shrugged. "Fine. I'll sit with you. And you need more than a drink. Just because you're a demigod doesn't mean you shouldn't eat. Take care of yourself."

"Thanks," I muttered.

"I'm just saying. I'll order food for you."

"Not a chance," I said. "Sit, Mary. And be glad that I'm not killing you for what you did to me the last time I saw you."

"Oh, that? Is that why you've been ignoring me the last fifty years?"

"Yes," I hissed.

She grinned, and I felt my entire being forgive her within a mere second.

"Darling, it's just part of the game." She pressed a button

that would call for service. "And why pay for this part of the train if you will not use their services?"

The door opened, the two of us looking up.

"Oh, good heavens," Mary sighed. "Why do they always look me in the eyes?"

The human turned to stone.

"Gods damn it, Mary. Every time I see you, there's trouble."

"Well, at least I'm exciting."

Pleasure pulled me from the dream. I groaned as I felt a wave of it rush through me, gasping as I opened my eyes. I glanced at the clock on the side table, seeing that it was 7am.

I felt a tongue swirling my clit, drawing another groan from me.

Fuck.

I reached under the blankets, curling my fingers in Madeline's hair. "Good girl," I huffed. "You know what daddy needs."

I groaned as she continued, pleasure rolling through me as her tongue thrust inside of me, followed by two slender fingers. I was still in a dreamy state, everything feeling absolutely perfect.

"Fuck," I moaned.

I arched against the bed as an orgasm crashed into me. My muscles coiled, every part of me tensing as the wave swept through me, followed by the mind-blowing relaxation.

She let out a satisfied hum. I dragged her up, pulling her on top of me to kiss her glistening lips.

"Morning," she whispered, kissing me again.

She rested her face between my breasts, melting on top of me. I smiled, running my palm up and down her back.

"I was dreaming about when you told me to make the Fates let me join the mafia," I said.

"Oh yeah," she sighed. "I forget I'm the reason you did. You never admitted that I was right."

"You were right," I chuckled.

She'd been correct about whatever demigods were left in the world. Aside from the five of us that had been picked, the others had perished.

It did not surprise me that Clotho would do the same to Madeline. They didn't see us as living beings. They only saw us as pieces of threads.

Once again, all I could think about was how I could stop the Fates from taking Madeline from me.

CHAPTER 13

FUCK FATE

P ercy

Paris and Ty sat across from me, their postures relaxed.

I wanted to slit their throats.

They were unbothered by my barely disguised hostility. This sort of tension was something we were all accustomed to within the Three Fates Mafia.

Madeline was wearing a gold glittering dress, her hair pulled back. She was stunning, alluring, deadly. There was a coffee table between us and them, four cups on it, with steam curling up.

Paris and Ty were twins, but they did not look alike. Paris had blonde hair and bright green eyes, a chiseled jaw, and a muscled body. In their monster form, he formed the lion-like part of their body.

Ty had jet black hair and dark mossy green eyes. If I didn't know better, I would have said he was a son of Hades. But he was a monster, and this mortal form was merely a gift from the Fates so that he could blend in with the rest of the world. He didn't have a mortal or human side to him, even if no one knew it.

Ty was taller and leaner than Pairs. He was quiet, his gaze thoughtful. He wouldn't speak unless he felt like it was actually important.

They were responsible for the deaths that occasionally happened near my clubs. A mortal they wanted to play cat and mouse with would stray too far from the sidewalk, their life becoming a game to them.

I hated the twins. They were mean motherfuckers.

I had fought with them on and off until the Fates had created the pact between our side and theirs, and there were still moments we'd stab each other in the back.

But, I was a demigod.

Madeline was not.

She gave them a slow, cruel smile. I loved it when she was like this. Calculating. Cold. Ruthless. I could be those things too, but when she sank her fangs into the truth, she would not let go.

"So. Are you going to admit to ransacking my apartment? Or something else?"

"We had nothing to do with your apartment," Paris said, offering her an imitation of a smile. "We know who did. But that information comes with a price."

"And what price is that? Since when do you betray your own kind?" she asked.

"I am not the one sitting next to a demigod, Medusa. You are."

Hate filled the silence. Venomous hate from all of us.

"Her name is Madeline," I said. "It is the name she has asked to go by, and yet you disrespect her."

"I've known her as Medusa since before you were born, daughter of Zeus," Paris said, his eyes blazing.

"I don't give a fuck."

Ty cocked his head, focusing on me. He was still silent.

I had to wonder if these two were the ones that had killed Diego. It still hurt when I thought of his death. It wasn't his time to go, and yet he was gone.

"Do you deny what I insinuate?" Paris asked.

"You left a card with a bartender in one of Perseus' bars. This bar is on the same block as my apartment, which was destroyed in the last three days. Based on the corpse that ruined my very expensive chair—which I will charge you for depending on your involvement—the intruder was there on Tuesday night. You have admitted to having information on this. Spill it."

"Or what?" Paris asked. "And are you not going to mention that the corpse belongs to one of *her* men?"

"Cerberus and the Colchian both owe me favors," Madeline continued. "They would help me destroy you."

"The Hydras don't," he said with ease. "Seeing as they supposedly saved your life. But I doubt you will live. That blade would have killed the Colchian, but he has two hearts. Has he told you that the other heart no longer works? You do not have such luck. You have a single heart. The Hydras are not magical, and yet they seem to have cured you." He leaned forward in his seat, picking up his cup of coffee. He had a smug expression. "Perhaps it was the demigod they have captured."

Alarm bells went off in my head. What the fuck was he talking about? Did they have a demigod imprisoned?

Madeline snorted, waving away his words. "Do you think I care if they have captured a demigod? Unlike you, I do not give a shit about their personal life. And yes, they helped me this week. That does not account for the many favors I have done for them. Do you want a war with me, Paris? Because I would squash the two of you like gum under my very expensive heels."

Ty growled. "You could try."

Another moment of silence.

"Percy, I am just having a hard time understanding why we came to meet you as well," Paris said lightly, taking a sip of coffee.

"Percy is my *mate*."

Paris choked and nearly spit, his shock genuine. It took every ounce of control not to burst out laughing. I looked over at Madeline, knowing she felt the same way.

If it were professional to fist bump her, I would have.

"What?" Paris asked.

"We are mates," I said.

I didn't know we were going to announce this to the entire world, but I wasn't against it. I was tired of hiding.

"Sanctioned by the Fates and everything. That is why you are here. Because if you harm my mate, or know something about what is trying to harm her, and you withhold that information—I can think of two demigods who would be happy to support me against you."

There was silence. Each side was trying to decide what move to make next. Each of us calculating.

Ty shifted in his seat, leaning forward. "You should tell them. This is not a game we want a part in, brother."

Even monsters respected mates. It was one of the few things our sides had ever agreed upon.

A vein throbbed in Paris' temple. He sighed, collecting himself. "Fine. Consider this a favor to you, *Madeline*. You owe us."

She didn't immediately respond. Instead, she reached for the coffee cup sitting in front of her. We watched her pick it up and take a sip. "Fine," she finally said. "Continue."

"There are monsters aside from us, as we all know. The Fates have blessed us, given a chance to live in the world which feared us for so long. We have wealth. We have power. Other creatures do not." He drummed his fingers on the arm of the chair. "About a week ago, there was a hit placed on Medusa by an anonymous party. They sent it out into the dark web, which alerted us. I'm certain that the Hydras knew, as well as Theseus and Orpheus."

"And none of you thought to mention this at our meeting last week?"

"It was after the meeting," he said. "I didn't think it was serious. Who would actually attack one of us? But then you were."

"By the Minoan Bull," I said.

"Yes. He has reasons to hate all of us. We did not rescue him from Jason."

"He's a murderer," I said.

"You know what I hate more than murderers? Liars," he seethed. I felt a flicker of panic. What if he knew what Clotho had said about Madeline? "Besides. We're all murderers. I can't fault him for that, and neither can you. You can't sit across from me, demigod, and pretend that your hands aren't as bloody as his."

"So, did you kill the man in her apartment?" I pressed, feeling a flicker of fury.

Part of me wanted it to be them. Then I could kill them without a second thought, right?

"No. But he was being stalked by a monster. There have been reports of three different ones. The bull, harpies, and cyclopes."

What the fuck were they all doing in our city? For the rest of the world, they could do whatever they wanted. But to set foot on our turf and cause problems was unacceptable.

I couldn't speak for Madeline necessarily, but I couldn't

understand why they would go after her. There was no reason
for that to be the case. From my understanding, she had always
helped other monsters. Especially ones that the Fates or gods
had forsaken. For them to turn on her like this was strange.

I could understand them killing one of my men. I knew that
being a demigod meant they did not like me. They had reasons
to hate me, and to hate the other elder demigods as well.
Orpheus, Theseus, Jason, Hercules, me. All of us had destroyed
their lives. We had killed other creatures just like them and then
were called heroes.

"Who put the hit out?" I asked.

"I don't know. The name was anonymous. It was simply the
letter C."

I suddenly felt sick.

Clotho.

Had Clotho placed a hit on Madeline? Were the Fates
really against us?

"You know who it is," Ty said, eyes glinting.

His words hung in the air like a guillotine. I felt Madeline
look at me, felt the heat in her gaze.

"Do you?" she asked.

I didn't answer. Part of me wondered if the Fates heard us
speaking now. Could they tell where my thoughts were, what I
wanted to do to keep Madeline alive?

"I don't," I lied.

"If one of them killed you, they would have a right to take
over your part of the mafia," Paris said to her, standing. He ran
his palms down his suit, arching a brow. "We are done here."

"Leave," she said, waving her hand.

Ty stood and followed his brother out the front door. I
followed behind them, locking it as soon as it shut.

It was time to tell the truth.

I turned around and met her gaze from across the room. She remained seated, her back straight and shoulders pulled back.

I approached her slowly and then sank to my knees on the floor in front of her. She blew out a breath, shaking her head.

"I knew it." Her voice trembled with rage. "I *knew* you were hiding something from me. I've known you for so long and I knew you were omitting something."

"You have every right to be angry with me," I said. "It's not something I wish to tell you."

She glared for a moment. My heart beat faster. I expected her to shout, maybe, or even want to fight me.

I would have been mad.

I would have been hurt.

Instead of any of that, she simply reached for me, cupping my face. "Tell me."

My breath left me.

I had been dreading this moment. Dreading telling her the truth. But, I couldn't hide it any longer.

The only way forward was by telling her everything.

"Clotho gave me a letter on Sunday. One that confirmed you are my mate, but also claimed you had one month to live. And so I wanted to find the knife so that I could fight her for you, or at the very least barter—"

"Are you insane?" She blinked at me and then shook her head, her grip tightening on my face. "You don't plot *against* the Fates, darling. That is how you end up in Tartarus, or worse."

"I don't care," I whispered, tears filling my eyes. I'd thought this through so many times, and every time my resolve only strengthened.

I would fight the Fates for her.

"I just told you that you are dying and you are worried about me?" I asked.

"Of course I am," she hissed. "You even thinking of challenging them is insanity. And no, I'm not happy you lied."

"I won't let them take you from me," I said. "I'll come with you to the underworld, if that's what it takes."

"Would Hades even let us be together?" she asked. "You're a hero. I'm a villain."

"You are *not* a villain," I growled. "You're not. You're nothing like the villains I have fought, Madeline."

"Darling, I am okay with being the bad guy," she snorted. "I've been *that bitch* for centuries. And I've enjoyed every moment of it. It's made my life a lot more entertaining and when you've been alive this long, that type of enjoyment is necessary."

"So, is that it, then? You're just going to accept your fate."

"Yes."

I couldn't live with that. We couldn't just let the Fates take her like this. I wouldn't let them do it.

I needed her.

She was right about finding enjoyment in life. Finding what made you happy, what made you tick.

She was that for me.

"I refuse to let them. We have to do something," I snarled. "We have to."

"We could mate. Like fully mate. At least then, the motherfuckers trying to steal my spot in the mafia wouldn't be able to. It would belong to you when I die."

My mouth fell open. I was both flattered and offended. I shook my head. "Mads, I have no interest in your part of the mafia. I never have."

"I know that. But I still prefer that it go to you. If I'm going to die, we might as well fuck everyone over on the way out. And I want you to scatter my ashes on that altar to Poseidon in Athens after you *destroy* it."

The corner of my mouth tugged. Our conversation horrified me, but of course she'd still want to give the finger to the gods.

"You know we could destroy that and still have you live."

She leaned in, her lips almost touching mine. Her eyes morphed into that of Medusa, the diamond pupils expanding in her golden irises. I swallowed hard, always enamored by how stunning she was.

"You know I could bite you and seal our mating bond. I bet you'd like the feel of my venom."

Exchanging blood and venom together would do it.

"I know I would," I whispered. "Fuck. I want to mate with you, but I want to save you. We can fight this. We're smart. We're powerful. We can destroy them, Mads."

We stared at each other for a moment.

"They're the Fates," she said. "I don't think we can destroy them."

"We can try."

If we were mated, our connection would become undeniable. I wasn't sure how our powers would fuse together, but I knew it would strengthen us. Ashley and Serena were still figuring their abilities out and their connections with their mates were already extraordinary.

"I'd rather we mate and enjoy our time together."

"What if we mate and then destroy everything instead?"

She fought off a smile. I could see it, her lips fighting the tug. I wanted to see her fangs.

"That sounds nice," she sighed. "We've always been enemies. What would happen if we weren't?"

"We'd win. I don't give a fuck if it's the Fates. I don't give a fuck if it's the gods. I will do anything to keep you, Madeline."

She rolled her eyes, but her cheeks flushed pink. "Are you proposing?"

"Yes. I say we mate and then raze the entire fucking city."

"That's not a bad idea. Sounds like a good way to celebrate."
We grinned at each other.

"I like it when you come to the dark side," she teased. "It's
nice to see a morally gray hero. One that I can devour."

"We both know that I will put you on your fucking knees,
kitten."

She leaned forward. Our lips touched lightly at first. Then
she slid her fingers into my hair, gripping me as we deepened
the kiss.

I could feel myself unraveling. Falling apart at the seams,
needing to fight the whole fucking world for her. And I would.
We would.

But right now, that wasn't what I wanted to think about.

I was going to finally get the girl.

She moaned, melting against me. I slid my hands up her
thighs and gripped them, nipping her bottom lip.

She changed as we kissed, something that she had never
done before. It was a fleeting thought, but I appreciated that she
was comfortable enough to change with me touching her. I
groaned against her as her dress ripped, her hips becoming
scaled and her wavy locks curling into serpents.

I pulled back, the two of us panting. I grabbed the bodice of
her dress and tore, ripping what was left of the fabric from her
body. She leaned back in her chair, her cheeks flushed as I
kissed her breasts. Her stomach, her hips, moving down to her
slit.

I pushed my tongue inside of her, drawing a sharp cry from
her. Her hips bucked against me, her head falling back as I
pushed two fingers inside of her. She was already wet and ready
for me.

"Fuck," she gasped.

Electricity rolled through me, all the way to the fingers I

thrust inside of her. I could control the current, keeping it low as I fucked her with my hand.

"Fuck. How are you doing that?"

I smiled, pressing the tip of my tongue against her clit as I continued. Her cries and moans intensified as I upped the intensity, using my ability to drive her crazy.

For the first time in a very long time, I was thankful to be a daughter of Zeus.

Chapter 14

Girl Dinner

M adeline

I screamed as the electricity *in my pussy* became more intense. She had shocked me, literally and figuratively, enough that all I could think about was *more.*

Yesterday, she'd given me a taste of her ability, but now she was giving me the full fucking meal.

My fingers curled into her silver hair. I held onto her as every muscle in my body wound up, a cry leaving me as I felt my first orgasm overwhelm me. She didn't let up, even as I came for her.

"Daddy," I panted.

She shifted forward, her electrical fingers still thrust inside me as her other hand slid up my body. I gasped as she wrapped it around my neck, giving me my favorite sort of necklace.

She squeezed, cutting off my breath. Our gazes met as she controlled me, used me, fucked me.

I felt myself melting right in front of her. Giving in completely. She was my mate; I knew it more than anything else. She was mine, and I was hers.

I didn't want to give that up.

A large shock rocked through my core. I couldn't suck in a breath, instead feeling like I was floating as I let go of all control.

I trusted her.

She eased her grip, allowing me to breathe for a moment. I sucked in a breath, my eyes fluttering. I ran the tip of my tongue over my fangs, the need to mate her becoming more and more urgent.

I needed to taste her blood. I needed her to taste mine. I wanted to give every part of myself to her, for the two of us to fuck and fuck through the frenzy this desire to mate was causing.

"Where do you want to mark me?" she asked.

"Where everyone in the entire fucking world can see." My voice was raspy, my words hungry.

"Come again for me first, kitten."

"Fuck," I whimpered.

The electricity rolled through my body, already edging me towards another orgasm. My nipples hardened, my wings spreading behind me as I tipped my head back.

"*Come*," she demanded harshly.

My body reacted to her command, an orgasm rushing through me. Pleasure flooded me, my eyes squeezing shut as I rode through the glorious wave.

"Good girl," she purred, pulling her fingers free.

She rose and began stripping. I watched her through my satisfied haze, admiring the morning sun caressing her tan skin. Light brushed her well defined muscles, her silver hair gleaming like starlight.

Percy stepped forward and straddled me. She swept her hair back, offering me her neck.

I felt tears blur my vision. The universe was finally giving us what we both deserved. Knowing that it might disappear made me savor this all the more.

"You're such a sap," she teased, her voice husky. "Bite me."

I leaned forward and sank my teeth into her neck. She sucked in a breath as my fangs broke her skin, and I groaned as her blood filled my mouth. My eyes closed, I sucked her in. Tasting her, drinking her. I could feel our bond already coming to life, the magic of finding the person who was yours, buzzing like a live wire.

Fuck. She tasted amazing. I took more of her blood, and I could feel my venom leaking from my fangs. She groaned again, her body grinding against mine.

I drew back, her blood wetting my lips. I licked them, looking up at her. She leaned down, kissing my neck before doing the same to me. I yelped as her blunt teeth broke my skin, a flare of pain followed by pleasure that was impossible to describe. My entire body felt like it had connected to hers, our powers blurring together.

My eyes closed as she sucked, drinking my blood the same way that I had taken hers. Mating this way made me feel like a vampire, but I could feel the bond strengthening as she took from me. She pulled back with a little grunt, licking her lips.

When I looked at her now, I could see all of her power. I could see the sheen of electricity around her body and the currents underneath her skin. Her eyes were bright blue, her strength breathtaking.

I wondered what she saw when she looked at me.

Her eyes softened. "You're beautiful," she whispered. "And you're mine. Mine forever."

"I am," I whispered.

I sniffled as she cupped my face gently. She kissed me, our heartbeats pounding in my ears. I listened, amazed, as they fell into sync.

She pulled back. The taste of our blood in my mouth. She slid off my lap and held out her hand. I took it, allowing her to pull me up.

A reverent silence settled between us. I felt like we were walking through a sacred place. She guided me through the house and up the stairs. My tail slithered behind us, my wings tucking behind my shoulders.

When I was with her in this form, I no longer felt like the monster that everyone hated. I felt loved. I felt cherished. And now that we had this bond between us, I could feel all of those things when she looked at me.

For a brief second, I could see myself through her eyes. And for the first time in a very long time, I loved myself.

I knew we had things we needed to do. I knew that the two of us had people to kill, and a city to search. A world to take over. But right now, all I could think about was being with her. Loving her, submitting to her.

She led me to the bedroom and pushed open the door.

"Stay here," she said. "Get on the bed and wait."

"Okay," I said.

I swallowed hard as I went to the bed, acutely aware of her movements. She went into the adjoining bathroom as I settled down on the soft mattress, adjusting myself until I was at the center. I spread my wings behind me. Her gardenia scent made my mouth water and suddenly, I was aware of the urge to turn this room into a nest.

Mating with her was awakening many primal urges, ones that I had a hard time denying. I was hot and desperate, every part of me yearning for her.

Percy came back holding a double-sided dildo and a bottle

of lube. The toy curved slightly, a bright pink silicone that would be soft and perfect for us to share.

All I could think about was what she would do to us with it.

Thoughts of her riding me, fucking me over and over, sharing it between us—they filled my mind, turning me on even more than I already was. I bit my lower lip as she climbed onto the bed, her gaze sultry and drawing me in.

She completely enthralled me. I could feel her heart beating with mine, could smell her arousal. She straddled my hips, running her palm over my stomach and the scales that began on the lower part, dipping down to my slit.

"Fuck," I groaned. "What are you going to do to me?"

"Heavenly things, kitten."

My nipples hardened as she smiled. The tone of her voice had cast a spell over me.

"You're so needy," she whispered. "I can feel how much you want me right now. It's like you've gone into heat."

I blushed. I didn't have words. I'd never felt like this before.

Leaning towards me, her lips almost touched mine. "I'm going to take care of us, kitten. I promise."

"Okay," I whispered, my voice faint.

"Thank you for trusting me."

I nodded, sucking in a breath as she uncapped the lube and poured some generously in her hand. She ran it up and down the toy; the liquid glistening and slick.

"This is the perfect toy for both of us. But if you don't like it, you have to tell me."

"Oh, I think I'm going to like it."

She smirked as she lowered one head towards my pussy, easing it inside. I groaned as she penetrated me, working it in slowly. I writhed beneath her, pleasure rolling through my body as she pulled it back and forth until I could take every inch.

She then lifted herself up, hovering over the other head of

the toy. I watched as she slowly lowered herself, her breath hitching as she took it.

Fuck. Her pussy was wet, her muscles tense as she worked herself up and down. Every movement sent another bolt of pleasure through me, the silicone cock moving between us.

"Daddy," I whined.

"You're my good girl," she praised. "You're taking this so well."

She took the rest of it, her head tipping back on a moan. I reached up, cupping her breasts as she moved her hips.

The two of us groaned together. Her hips rolled, the toy moving between us. My hands fell down to the blankets, my talons ripping the fabric. I tensed as we moved against each other, my hips rocking against hers.

Pleasure rolled through both of us, and I loved the feeling of being closer to her. Of being with her. I could feel our needs through our bond, the freshly mated link echoing our desires.

I parted my lips on a cry, the edge of an orgasm building and building. She planted her hands on my chest, her gaze locking with mine as she ground against me harder.

Years of yearning and wanting and needing had all led to this moment. Of the two of us being together, accepting each other. Finally, succumbing to the truth.

That she belonged to me. And I belonged to her.

Electricity ran over her skin, bright blue flashing through the room. There was a storm between us, growing and growing as we both tumbled towards the edge.

Sweat gleamed on her tan skin, her silver hair floating around her. I dug my talons into her thighs, the taste of her blood still on my tongue.

"I'm going to come," I gasped.

"Me too."

We kept going until finally, we both cried out, coming

together at the same time. My back arched, my pussy gripping the cock as I came hard.

I could feel her pleasure, too. My eyes fluttered as I relaxed into the bed, the two of us panting. She moaned, collapsing forward and pressing her head against my breasts.

She lifted her hips, pulling the toy out between us and tossing it to the side of the bed. She melted against me, her legs tangling with my tail as we relaxed.

Everything felt perfect when I was with her.

"How do you feel?" she murmured.

"Amazing," I whispered. "And you?"

She chuckled, looking up at me. "You already know. You can feel it."

"True." I smiled as she rolled off me.

I shifted back into my mortal form so that my wings wouldn't get in the way as she spooned me. She pulled me against her body, her arms curling around my waist.

Her fingers traced light circles against my skin, silence settling between us. I closed my eyes, listening to the rise and fall of her breath. Feeling the way she fit against me, the smoothness of her skin against mine.

The Fates couldn't take this from me.

I'd lived too long. I'd done too much. And I didn't understand why they would suddenly turn against me.

"Who was the Fate that spoke to you?" I asked.

"I don't want to talk about that now," she sighed.

"I know. But remind me..."

"Clotho."

I frowned. Rash decisions were unlike Clotho. The Fates had also never told someone of their ending before, at least that I knew of.

Something about this entire situation felt wrong, but I

couldn't quite understand it yet. We didn't have enough information. We didn't have the answers yet.

"We need to meet with everyone," I sighed.

"Is this like a post-nut epiphany?"

I barked out a laugh and rolled over, our noses touching.

"What do we know so far? We know that someone is out to kill me. We know that the Minoan Bull stabbed me with that knife. We know that the knife is supposedly the reason I'm going to die. But that knife didn't kill you when you were stabbed at the gala. That knife didn't kill Ian. And if that knife is supposed to kill anything, then why didn't it kill either of you?"

"Well, I'm a demigod."

"Yes, but that knife kills *everything*."

"It also stabbed my leg. And my leg still aches sometimes."

"I think Orpheus is a fucking liar, and the knife doesn't kill everything. Myths and legends hold power. If none of us knew the truth..."

"But what about you? You are dying. You are supposed to die, according to Clotho. What if the legend is true, but it's conditional?"

I frowned. I could feel my thoughts turning, trying to spin together the web of deceit. What reason would the Minoan Bull have to kill me? I had no issues with him. And he had clearly been angry when he had stabbed me. Someone was pulling the strings. Someone was sending other monsters after me, turning them against one of their own.

Not to mention, the whole situation with Diego was strange. Why had he been in my apartment? Why had he died the way he had? It was unlike anyone nowadays to put drachmas inside a dead body.

Everything was chaos. Nothing quite fit together, but I knew that just meant there were missing pieces.

"Perhaps you should pray to the gods," I muttered.

"I stopped that a long time ago. They don't answer us. They don't care."

I agreed there. But she was a demigod. Surely, Zeus could not forever ignore his own child.

"What if it's one of us that's doing this?" I asked.

She mumbled something under her breath and then cupped my face. "Give me two minutes of absolute blissful silence and then we will work. Okay? I'm still riding the high of my orgasm."

I grinned and nodded. "Deal."

At the end of the two minutes, she let out a very long sigh and then sat up. She reached across the bed, grabbing a hair-band from the side table and pulling her hair up into a loose bun.

"I say we take a long hot bath and discuss."

"Wonderful."

Within a few minutes, the two of us were settling into her massive bathtub with a bottle of champagne, a plate of crois-sants balanced on the edge, and hot water running with Epsom salts.

"If it is one of them, then we should be able to find out easi-ly," Percy said. She turned off the running water as it finished filling and then picked up her bubbling drink. "A toast," she said, tilting the glass forward. "To being badass mafia bitches who are in love."

Love. My heart skipped a beat, but I picked mine up and clinked it with hers. She somehow made me feel like a teenage girl again, every part of me squealing on the inside. "To being badass mafia bitches."

We both drank. I hummed, sinking into the hot water with a happy sigh. It was hard to keep focusing on our problems. And hell, at least I got to think about them like this.

"We could call a meeting," Percy said. "And press for

answers. We could push for having access to all the parts of the city. We'd be able to tell a lot from that."

"We would," I agreed. "Are there any gods that hate you? Or goddesses?"

Percy frowned. "I mean, I'm sure there are several that don't like me. But I'm not aware of any direct hate. We are nothing but ants to them."

"I think we're more like butterflies. They *do* watch," I sighed.

"Why do you ask?"

I shrugged and reached for one croissant, tearing off a piece. "Just thinking."

Gods and goddesses were fickle. It wouldn't take much for them to interfere and make our lives hell. But I couldn't think of any sleight Percy or I might have done.

"I think Eric might have a lead on the bull." She let out a heavy sigh and tipped her head back on the edge of the tub. "I'll talk to him after we finish here. Then we can call a meeting for tomorrow. Depending on the outcome of those two events, we can go hunting. Truly hunting."

"They won't stand a chance." I took a bite of the croissant and then leaned back. "I'll paint the whole fucking city red."

"You and me both."

"So, tomorrow we meet everyone. Figure out if one of them is causing issues. We get free rein in Moirai. And then we hunt down the assholes trying to kill me, find the knife, and then what?"

"I use the knife to kill Clotho."

My mouth fell open, the champagne glass nearly slipping from my fingers. I stared at her, wondering if the two of us would be struck down here and now.

She lifted her head, looking directly at me. "If she won't let you live, then she can go to the underworld. It's simple."

"You can't fight her."

"I can and will."

"You've lost your mind."

"Perhaps. I don't even care. I don't want to be here without you."

"You're willing to give up everything?" I asked. "Everything you've worked for? Everything you've done?"

"What have I worked for, Mads? I'm not an artist like you. I'm not a painter or writer. I don't have a family. I don't have any pets unless you count Elektra. I'm not a hero anymore, but I'm also not retired. I don't even know what I'm doing with my life."

I scoffed and moved closer to her; the water sloshing around me. "You're a badass mafia bitch. You run a business, an organization. You help people when you can. Don't pretend we both don't know how you donate your money."

Her cheeks flushed. "You shouldn't know that."

"Yeah, and you shouldn't have a key to my apartment."

She snorted. I narrowed my eyes at her gaze, wondering what else she had of mine.

"You're selling yourself short," I said. "And you've lived this long without me."

"Mads, I've been living this long *for* you."

I rolled my eyes. "Now you're just being dramatic."

"I'm serious. I've wanted you since the moment I washed up on your beach."

"You know, I wanted to kill you then," I sighed. "Gods, that was so long ago. And then over the years..."

"We've always come back to each other."

And that was the truth.

My heart skipped a beat, and I blushed, thinking about the past. About all the things we'd done. We'd fought to stay alive in a world where we were nothing but relics. Adapting, killing, fighting, fucking.

But never loving.

Not until now.

I couldn't even bring myself to say it aloud. I feared the Fates would hear us. But Percy, being her, already seemed to read my mind.

"It'll be a deal or no deal situation. I won't budge. If they take you, Mads, they take me too. We're mates now."

"I don't know how we can be so romantic and apocalyptic at the same time."

"Perks of being myths and legends in the flesh."

I fought the urge to roll my eyes again, instead leaning forward more. She leaned forward too, our knees knocking against each other.

"Percy," I whispered. "There's no way you can stop her."

She held up her hand, offering it to me.

"I'll make a bet. If I stop her, then you have to wear a collar that says *"She is my god and I bow to her"*."

My mouth fell open. "I absolutely will not."

"Then take the bet since you're so sure."

Was I really going to bet against us winning?

I slid my hand into hers, bubbles dripping from our grip. I shook it, doing my best to ignore the way my stomach twisted.

I hoped I was wrong.

But it was rare that I ever was.

There was a very real possibility that I was going to the Underworld and she was coming with me. I didn't like the idea of her suffering because of me.

"We'll be okay," she said. "I look forward to fucking you with that collar on."

"Are you going to make me bow down to you?"

"Absolutely."

Of course.

I couldn't say I hated that idea, despite my protesting.

"When we survive this, take me to your studio," she said. "You can sculpt me. I may not have the tits of a nun, but they're still nice."

I grinned at her. "I'd like that. Does that mean I get to tell you what to do?"

She raised a brow. "We'll see."

I could make a whole exhibit just with sculptures of her.

I had a flicker of hope. One that I was doing my best to stop from becoming a wildfire.

It was better to be surprised than hope we'd get to spend the rest of our lives together.

"Tomorrow," she said. "Tomorrow, we will get answers."

CHAPTER 15

DIVISION

P ercy

Eric pulled our car up to what appeared to be an abandoned building. On the outside, it was rundown and discreet, but on the inside—it held the place where the Three Fates Mafia leaders met. Everyone had agreed to meet with us, despite some grumbles here and there.

It helped that Madeline had insisted it was urgent.

I glanced over at her, admiring her appearance. Her dark hair was in a chignon, her black dress concealing several knives.

"You look beautiful," I said.

"Thank you." She winked at me from behind her sunglasses.

"How do I look?" I asked.

"Positively ominous," she teased. "Very threatening. I think the suit helps. You look better in one than any of the men in there."

I smiled. That was the best compliment I could ask for, especially with the mood I was in.

I opened the door and stepped out, holding it open for Madeline. She got out of the car, the two of us heading for the doors. Two security guards that stood there opened them for us.

We stepped inside and strode down the long, frigid hallway. I could feel the others behind the doors at the very end.

"Are we sure we want to do this?" she asked.

"Yes," I said. "I want to make sure that none of them have anything to do with what has been happening. And I will look this time. Especially at Orpheus and Theseus."

Orpheus had agreed to come, which was a surprise. He clearly had his own agenda, one that I had a feeling would interrupt my own. It didn't matter, though. Not right now. What I needed to make sure of was that if any of them were involved, we would make it known they would suffer.

And if they weren't, then truly I could turn my sights on to the Fates and the strangers that were invading our city.

Eric had a lead about the bull. I was certain he was staying in the center of Moirai in the basement of a rundown bar no one ever went to. To the humans, he appeared to be an attractive man. To us, we would know the truth.

The Minoan Bull had never been my enemy until this last week. Unfortunately for him, that would mean his end was upon him.

I would kill him for what he did to the woman who belonged to me.

I stepped into the meeting room, feeling everyone's gaze turn to me. Madeline followed behind me, and I felt the urge to sneer as all of their eyes turned to her. When I was with her, I felt increasingly protective over her.

We called the Three Fates Mafia together again for two reasons.

One, I wanted to clarify that *she* was mine.

And two, I wanted to see if I could figure out if any of them had something to do with everything happening.

Ashley and Serena were here, too. I gave them both a quick glance before sitting down.

Paris smirked, raising a brow at me. I knew all of them could see our mating marks.

Orpheus looked like he was about to blow. Theseus appeared curious.

The rest of them simply stared.

"Well," Ian said, clearing his throat. "This is completely unexpected, but congratulations."

"Thanks," Madeline said. "We're happy, of course."

"How long has this been going on?" Orpheus gritted out.

"Us together, or us working against everyone else?" I quipped. I gave him a fake smile. "Just joking, of course. Besides, we're not here because we are mated. We are here for entirely different reasons."

"We can't just glaze over the fact the two of you are mates," Damon said. "This is shocking."

"Why? Because we're women?" Madeline asked. She leaned back in her chair, crossing one leg over the other. She regarded him coldly.

"No. For fuck's sake," he growled. "None of us in this room are the picture of a 'traditional' relationship. Because *you're* Medusa and *she's* Perseus. This is different. There is a history here we can't simply ignore."

"It's not any different from us," Ashley said to him. She also looked at Minos and Aaecus, an unspoken agreement passing between their side. "Percy and Madeline have a right to be happy, too. It doesn't matter that she's not a 'new' demigod. We do not know what the Fates have planned."

My stomach twisted, although I appreciated her interjection. This was why I needed her and Serena at meetings. She was correct. None of us knew what the Fates might plan for us.

We didn't know if they would give us life or death. Happiness or sorrow.

Madeline pointed at her with an amiable smile. "You and Serena aren't allowed to miss meetings again. You should have been here for the shit show last week."

Serena snorted, giving everyone a loathing look. "Oh, we both heard about it."

"You are an *elder* demigod," Orpheus snarled. "You shouldn't be mated to a monster."

"I should have been mated to her centuries ago," I argued. "Your opinions are archaic and misguided, Orpheus. This is a new world, one where we don't have to heed the laws of kings or queens. I can love who I want. She can love who she wants."

"They are our enemies."

"They haven't been our enemies for a long time," I argued. "Well, perhaps they have been *your* enemies. But I think we can say that about more than just monsters."

His ears turned red. The tension in the room was already becoming insufferable. Madeline let out a low growl and for a moment, I wondered if she'd rip off the glasses she wore and turn him to stone.

I would have enjoyed that.

"You said this was urgent," Damon reminded us.

"I did," I said. "Someone is trying to kill Madeline. Someone has put out an anonymous hit on her, and because of that, several rogue monsters have invaded Moirai to kill her. I want them caught. And I want them slaughtered. In order to do so, I want us to have complete access to your territories without question for the next two weeks."

"Just because they are after her doesn't mean any of us should interfere," Argos said. "Besides. There are two of you now, *correct?* Use your own resources. We have no reason to help you."

"The fact is, all of you either owe me or Madeline a favor," I said.

"We paid our favor," he argued. "Last weekend, in fact."

"You can either comply or I will let the room know of the rumors I've heard about what treasure you hold inside your pretty mansion, Argos."

His eyes lit up with rage. Pierce and Bash tensed next to him, the three of them staring at me like a cornered but angry animal.

Interesting.

It was true then.

I gave a passing glance to Paris and Ty. Their expressions were unreadable.

"You could have said please," Argos growled, his voice laced with hate.

"When was the last time *you* ever said please?" Madeline snorted. "I really think the two of us are over pleasantries."

I turned my head and looked at Serena, but Ian held up his hand. "We will help. You don't need to look at our side that way. You helped us before, not to mention I do not want rogue monsters in our city. They are violating contracts by being here. It's our territory, not theirs."

"If all you are asking of us is to go into our territories without issues, fine," Theseus said.

All of us looked at him. He rarely spoke at meetings.

He shrugged. "That's all I have to say."

"Fine," I said. "Thank you."

"I wouldn't."

Cryptic as always.

"The bull still has my knife," Orpheus said. "I want my blade."

Minos groaned, leaning back in his chair. "Dude, we are all really fucking tired of listening to you bitch about your fucking knife. No one gives a fuck."

No one except me. I'd told him I'd give him the knife back when I found it, but that was now a lie.

Orpheus stood up abruptly, his chair screeching. "I should gut you for saying that, you stupid mutt."

Damon and Aaecus growled, but Ashley let out a low laugh. "Orpheus, I think we've all come to find you're all bark and no bite, so sit the fuck down."

That earned a series of mirthless chuckles.

"We have one other question," Madeline said, drawing everyone's attention again. She didn't even look up at them. She was studying her manicure, her aura of disdain turning me on.

I liked it when she did this. I enjoyed seeing her control the room.

"Are any of you behind these attacks?"

The room was silent. Her abruptness almost made me laugh, but now was not the time to do that. I could feel her amusement through our bonds, though, and that delighted me.

"None of us are," Serena said. "At least on this side of the table. I can't speak for the others."

"I can speak for us as well. We have nothing to do with any attacks," Ashley said, glancing at her three mates. They all nodded.

I looked around the room.

"We aren't behind this," Argos said, leaning back in his seat. He was clearly still pissed about my comment earlier.

"Neither are we," Paris said, gesturing at his twin. "We're monsters too."

My gaze swept to Theseus. "I'm not," he said. "I hardly have time to go after someone like *her*."

Orpheus was last then. He was fuming, his rage evident in

the way smoke was practically coming out of his ears. Corded veins throbbed in his neck, his fingernails digging into the table-top. "Do you really think I would?"

"It's a yes or no question."

We glared at each other. My pulse raced the longer we stared. Not because I feared him. Not because I worried about what he might do. But because he hadn't said no yet.

"Answer the question, Orpheus," Paris demanded. "Did you put out a hit on Medusa?"

"If one more fucking person calls her *Medusa*, I'm going to put a bullet through your head," I snarled. I still didn't break my eye contact with Orpheus despite the threat.

I felt Madeline's hand on my arm. The touch was casual, but immediately soothed me.

"The answer is no," Orpheus said. I didn't believe him. "This meeting was a waste of time."

He stood up and shoved the chair back fast enough that it toppled over. It was like watching a toddler kick over a tower of blocks. He marched out of the room, slamming the door behind him hard enough that the walls trembled.

"I fucking hate that guy," Minos muttered.

"As do I," Paris agreed.

Theseus stood too. "I'm done here. I may not agree with his reaction, but you have divided us, Perseus."

"Just get out," Madeline snapped. "For fuck's sake, you're annoying. And you smell weird."

He left swiftly. The moment the door closed again, there was an audible breath released in the room.

"I'm just going to say it," Damon said. "This room is what the future looks like. Or what it can look like."

"One can hope," I said, meeting his gaze.

"Percy, you've never been like them," Ian said. "Even centuries ago. We've all done terrible things here, and still do them. But I can understand why the Fates finally brought the two of you together."

Madeline and I were talented actresses, as always. None of them knew just how much his words made me want to vomit.

The Fates had brought us together at a price. One I wasn't willing to pay.

"Thank you, Ian," I said calmly. "We will hunt tonight."

Hunting, killing, and bringing everything closer to the end.

Chapter 16

Drachmas

M adeline

The moon shone high above the city, but the clouds and light emanating from Moirai blurred the stars. I breathed in the smog, the scent of filth, and the faint edge of salt from the ocean.

Hundreds of years to improve, but cities still disgusted me. At least the mortals had figured out better hygiene practices.

Percy stood next to me, as still as a statue. I didn't understand how she did it. I wanted to pace, to fidget, to move—but she insisted we stay right here.

I stole a glance at her. Her silver hair was pulled back tight. She wore a black turtleneck and slim pants with combat boots. Meanwhile, I only wore a backless tunic and weapons strapped to my body. I was in my monster form, my wings spread behind me and my long tail curled. I could feel the wind against us, the breeze holding a frigid edge.

"What if the lead is wrong?" I asked. "What if he's not here?"

"Then we will deal with it. We will find him, Mads."

Across from this ledge was the roof of another building. Between us, there was a dark alley with a door at the bottom. There was a red neon sign that burned like the mark of Hades. It felt as though we were looking down into Tartarus.

If what Eric said was true, we might get answers tonight. According to Percy's men, there had been a couple of sightings of the Minoan Bull, and all paths led to here.

The goal was to take captives, although I expected there to be casualties.

I didn't care.

Part of me wanted to burn down the building now. Did it matter if there were innocent people inside? I wasn't sure if it mattered to me as much as it did Percy.

"Eric and my men will be back up," Percy said. "Elektra will be around for an easy escape if things go south. We go in, we capture, we find out what's going on. We need to know two things. Where the bull is, because he has the knife. And who they were hired by so that we know who wants to kill you."

"Darling, this isn't my first rodeo."

"I know," she breathed out. "It's been a while since I've gotten my hands dirty."

"I can think of a few other times recently."

She snorted.

The sound of the door swinging open below drew our attention. I watched as a man stepped out into the cool night. He lit a cigarette, the butt burning bright orange as he inhaled.

Another figure moved behind him, one that was barely discernible to the eye. It was like a shadow, but I still saw it.

Percy and I were deadly silent. We watched as the being

went through the door. The man then put out his cigarette and turned, going back inside.

Percy moved in a blur, leaping over the side of the building. She landed and stopped the door from shutting, all in the blink of an eye.

I raised a brow. I'd forgotten that demigods were *actually* powerful.

I jumped off the ledge, my wings slowing my descent. I hit the ground and moved quickly as she opened the door. Our gazes locked as she drew her lightning bolt.

"I'll go in first," she whispered, ducking through the doorway.

I followed her. The scent of monsters was strong here, the air thick, an eeriness that practically crawled over my skin. If I didn't know any better, I would think we were going to the underworld—not inside some dinky hell hole in the middle of the city.

Percy moved quickly ahead of me. The hall was long, leading to a set of rusty doors at the end.

I can feel your unease.

Percy's voice filled my mind, surprising me. She paused in her steps, glancing over her shoulder at me.

Well, that's fucking cool.

Ew, you're in my mind, I hissed at her.

She snorted, but continued on. We stopped at the door at the end, taking a heavy pause.

I'd never worried about anyone else in a fight before now.

She kicked the door, and it burst open.

There were monsters here. There were men. All of them sat around what looked like a poker table, although instead of poker chips, there were drachmas. Two harpies, the shadow creature— a Shade—that we'd seen moments ago, and then their men.

But no bull.

Fucking hell.

"Perhaps the gods do care for us," the Shade rasped.

Percy raised her bolt. "We're looking for the Minoan Bull. We'll leave peacefully if you tell us where he is."

One harpy laughed. It was an annoying laugh, too. "Sorry, but the price on *her* head is worth more than our lives."

"Well, then I guess we'll do this the hard way," she sighed.

Everyone moved at once. My senses kicked in as she drew her bolt, the two of us already moving in the dance of a fight.

The harpies bared their fangs and rushed toward me. They had massive feathered wings and long hands that ended in sharp talons, their bird-like bodies moving swiftly. Both of them had the face of a woman, but everything else was monstrous.

I could just lift my glasses, but it had been a while since I'd had a good fight. And I was fucking sick and tired of everything that had happened this week.

I was going to mop their blood up with their raggedy hair.

The two of them charged me. I whipped two knives out, wielding them with ease. There was a flurry of wings and movement, their snapping teeth loud in my ears as I drove a blade into one of their necks. Blood spurted, a dark inky color that burned when it touched the flesh.

I sucked in a breath, swirling around and catching the other harpy with my blade. It wasn't fatal though, and she moved out of the way just in time before I could catch her with the other.

Pain flared from part of my tail. I glanced back, seeing her sink her talons into my scales. A growl ripped from me, the snakes around my head hissing. I was going easy on these bitches, and this was how they repaid me. I tossed the knife and ripped off my glasses.

She closed her eyes just in time.

A villainous laugh bubbled up from me. I glanced across the

room, seeing that Percy had already put three men on the floor and was now fighting the Shade.

"I can still fight, even without seeing," the harpy snarled.

"Percy," I called. "That's not how you fight a Shade."

Her lightning bolt was no use on it. I watched them fight, my stomach twisting.

"Percy!"

"I hear you!" she growled. "Watch yourself!"

I moved out of the way just as the harpy lunged for me again. I turned and twisted, moving to the side as her claws raked through the air.

Her talons dug further into my tail. I let out a little hiss, ignoring the bolt of pain as I grabbed her by her hair and slammed her down.

Out of the corner of my eye, I noticed more movement. But I focused on the monster I was fighting, the two of us tangled together.

I felt the bullet before I heard it. My body jerked back as it went through my shoulder, a sharp agony rendering me immobile. The harpy slammed me down onto the floor.

I hissed, my tail wrapping around her body as she went for my throat. I squeezed as hard as I could, my muscles snapping her bones. Her eyes bulged, her strength almost matching my own.

But not quite.

I wrenched my knife and thrust it through her chest. She screeched, falling back. Her blood sprayed over me and the floor. Pain seared me, her blood burning. I hissed, thankful that I healed faster than humans.

I released her, allowing her to flail. My skin closed back up where the blood had hit me.

Percy let out a sharp growl, and then suddenly the room lit up with an electric blur.

I could feel the power through my scales, but it did not hurt me the same way it did the others. I watched as everyone in the room collapsed except the two of us, even the Shade.

Silence followed.

Percy was covered in sweat and blood. Her chest was heaving, her pants loud.

"Fuck," she cursed. "It's been too long since I've gotten into a fight. They were annoying me."

"Me too," I growled. "Is everyone dead?"

"No. I used my electric shock to temporarily stop their hearts, and it made them pass out. They'll be waking up soon, so we need to tie them up. I'm going to call Eric and the rest of the men in if you don't mind putting your sunglasses back on..."

She rushed over to me, pulling me up. She cupped my face, her eyes flickering to the bullet that was still in my shoulder.

"Are you okay, kitten?"

"Just a bullet wound, darling," I said. "Nothing that I haven't had before and can't handle. My body will push it out and then the wound will heal quickly."

She nodded, releasing a breath. I watched her shoulder visibly relax.

"Were you worried about me?" I asked.

Her brows pinched together, but she didn't answer. Instead, she picked up my sunglasses and put them on me.

"Come on," I teased. "I'm tough."

"You are." She pulled me into an ardent kiss. I groaned against her, completely aware of the fact that they were still bodies around us.

She pulled back and pressed her forehead to mine. Her voice was husky as she spoke. "I'm going to call the boys in. We're going to take these monsters captive, and then when they wake up, we will find out more about the bull."

I nodded, holding onto her for a moment longer before releasing her.

She did exactly what she said. Within a minute, her men were swarming the room. They worked together to tie up the men and the monsters, binding them thoroughly so that they wouldn't be able to escape. I took a moment to look around the room, noting the walls were coated with specks of blood. The concrete floor was stained despite the bleach used in attempts to clean it. The green poker table at the center was covered in Greek drachmas, the cards appearing to be old.

What had they been doing here? And why had there been mortals involved?

I moved closer to the table, eyeing everything carefully. I picked up one of the coins, turning them over.

These are strange.

It has been ages since I had held a real one of these. I studied the metal, and the engravings on the front and back. It took me a moment, but then I realized that these were not true drachmas.

"What the fuck is going on?" I whispered to myself.

I could feel my body already beginning to heal as I stood there. I glanced at my shoulder, watching as the bullet slowly pushed itself from my muscles. It fell to the floor, the wound already healing. That, at least, was a good sign. Perhaps the knife hadn't hurt me as much as we thought.

I reached for the cards that were spread out over the velvet table. I picked one up, frowning at the texture of the card. I recognized it, but I couldn't quite place it.

"Mads," Percy called.

I looked up, raising a brow.

Our captives were now waking up. They were all tied together. Even the Shade was bound. I wondered where they'd gotten a chain that could hold him. I crossed the room to Percy, studying them.

One of the men's eyes fluttered, and he looked up.

Percy let out a little growl, leaning in and grabbing his jaw. Her knuckles turned white, her gaze boring into his.

"Where is the bull?" she asked.

He remained silent.

She backhanded him almost hard enough to crack his jaw. He let out a warbling noise, his eyes widening in pain. "I asked you a question," she said. "Where is he?"

"I'm not talking," he snapped.

"Eric, hand me a knife."

Eric passed her one. I watched as she brought the blade to the corner of his mouth, blood dripping down his skin.

"Talk or die," she sneered.

I'd never seen her so tense before. I could feel her rage through our mate bond, could feel the way she wanted to gut him.

All because of me.

Somehow, that turned me on.

He pissed himself.

All of us sighed as it pooled on the floor. He started to say something, and then I caught a familiar scent.

Percy and I both immediately turned.

We caught a fleeting glimpse of the Minoan Bull in the doorway before he took off running the other way.

"I'm going after him," she snarled.

"Percy!"

"Stay here. Don't follow."

"Percy—"

"Let me do this," she growled.

We stared for a split second. I nodded, letting her go.

"Thank you. I'll be back later," she said, taking off.

I watched as she ran after him, leaving me alone with her men and our captives.

Eric winced. "I...I'm not sure what we do now."

I thought about following her for a moment, but it was clear she wanted to track him herself. I stared at the doorway for a moment, contemplating what I wanted to do. I felt her rage. I felt how much anger she had at those that we had tied up. Plus, I was pissed too. I wanted answers from the motherfuckers that had been hunting me.

"Take them to wherever you keep people," I said, waving my hand. "I'll come with you. And get me a bottle of champagne to go with the torture. A nice one."

"Yes, Mistress."

I trusted Percy would catch him. She trusted I would handle the rest.

I'd drink champagne and torture the monsters that had tried to kill me.

She'd catch the one that had started it all.

Truly, the two of us made the best team.

CHAPTER 17

POWER

P ercy

I grabbed the bull by the horns and slammed him down onto the concrete.

I'd chased him up onto the roof of a building nearby, finally cornering him. The bastard was fucking massive and strong, but he was too big.

I was faster. Nimbler.

He twisted around, rolling the two of us. I wrapped my arm around the crook of his neck with a snarl, squeezing.

"One more move and I'll fucking fry you like a goddamned piece of meat," I huffed.

He stopped moving, the two of us panting.

"You have this all wrong, demigod," he growled. "I'm not the reason for any of this. I was hired."

"Where is the fucking knife?"

"They stole it from me," he rasped. "And the only reason I

had it in the first place was because it was given to me. They hired me to do this so that I could get a mortal cloak."

"You are the reason she might die," I seethed.

I was trembling. My emotions were unsteady, my rage pumping through me, giving me tunnel vision. He was the reason I had to fight the Fates. He was the reason all of this had started.

His breath sputtered as my grip tightened. "I can tell you who hired me if you let me live."

I snarled, tightening my grip as I thought that through. I couldn't let him live. Not after everything. Not after what we'd already been through.

"I—am—not—your—enemy."

"FUCK!" I shouted, but I released him.

I rolled to my feet, but he stayed put, laying flat on the concrete. We were the only two up here on the roof. The sun was breaking over the horizon.

"If you're lying to me—"

"I'm not," he huffed. "I don't want to die, but I needed that mortal cloak. I have been gone from this world for a long time, since Hercules captured me."

"I heard." I glowered at him, but ultimately rolled back onto my butt, sitting. "She is my mate."

"I know," he sighed.

"I have no sympathy for you."

"I wouldn't either. But I will tell you everything. I should start from the beginning."

"I don't need your fucking life story," I snapped. "I need to know who hired you. Demigod? Monster?"

"Orpheus. It was Orpheus. He stole his blade from Ian and then hired me to stab Madeline. But he said he was only following instructions." His voice lowered. "I don't know who else is behind this, but it runs deep. He was merely a middleman. He offered me a human form and a seat at the table if she died."

"I don't know why the fuck you'd want to be in the Three Fates Mafia."

"Are you kidding? Wealth, power, and the ability to be amongst mortals without them running in fear? It's a step up from being trapped in a hole on a beach for centuries. And before that, always running. Always fighting. You're a demigod, so you don't understand what we go through."

"You are on really thin ice right now."

He sighed and lifted his head, his horns gleaming. Smoke curled from his nostrils, his eyes burning like hot coals. "Are you going to kill me?"

"If I don't kill you, then you will owe me your life."

"I can live with that."

I snorted. I couldn't believe I was letting him live.

I could understand why he'd taken the offer.

"Orpheus then."

"Yes. But beyond him, I don't know."

There were many things wrong with this situation. Orpheus didn't work for others. Orpheus also would not have parted with the knife willingly.

Which meant that *other* was someone he couldn't say no to.

Had Clotho really orchestrated this entire situation? What if the Fates were truly behind everything?

"Why have you been evading us then?" I asked.

"I knew you wanted to kill me. And you aren't the only one," he grunted. "Am I free to go?"

"Yes, but don't leave the city. I might need you for something and now you owe me. Because I *was* going to kill you."

He got to his hooves and nodded. I watched as his form slowly changed from that of a massive Minotaur to just a man.

One that was buck naked.

I averted my eyes, making a face. "Go the fuck away."

"Thank you for sparing me."

"Leave," I growled.

And he did.

I sighed and laid back on the concrete, staring up at the sky. Madeline was safe for the moment. We'd captured everyone that had been inside that hellish room, and Eric had them imprisoned.

She had taken a bullet. But she was okay.

I was torn between absolute rage and absolute despair. A merry-go-round that wouldn't stop spinning in my mind.

"You look defeated."

My eyes widened, and I sat up abruptly. A chill settled over me as I met the gaze of Zeus.

Fuck.

What the fuck?

He looked like a normal man, although there was nothing normal about him. His skin rippled, trying to contain his form. His eyes were electric blue, the wind picking up around us.

"I am not defeated," I said, getting to my feet.

"Good. I would expect nothing less of my child."

I curled my lip as rage rolled through me. "Seriously? It's been centuries since you've spoken to me, and this is what you have to say?"

"Don't take that tone with me, child."

"I am not a *child*," I snarled.

The air crackled with electricity. I wasn't sure if it was from him or from me.

"I am here to warn you," he said. "And I urge you to heed the warning. You must let her die."

I stared at him now. I hadn't seen my father in centuries, and suddenly he showed up to tell me I had to let my mate die?

Absolutely not.

I didn't care that he was a god.

I didn't care that he could literally turn me into dust if he wanted to. I was *not* going to let her die. I didn't care who I had to fight. Who I had to kill. Who I had to piss off.

The gods could kiss my ass.

I was done playing these games. Done doing their bidding. I was no longer their pawn.

"There are more things happening here than what you can see," he said. "I do not want to see you perish because of another."

"She is my mate," I said. "I can't let her die. Surely you can understand that."

"You have to," he said. "You cannot fight everyone, Perseus."

Hearing him say my name made me feel nauseated. For him to stand there and tell me these things...

"I don't care if I go with her," I said. "I will fight to the very end for her. You could help me if you loved me."

He didn't say anything. But he didn't have to. I knew the gods weren't capable of love the same way that we were. And that was why I was glad I was a demigod. There was still a mortal part to my soul, a humanity that would never leave me.

It meant that I hurt more, and meant that I suffered more, but it also meant that I loved more.

He was not capable of caring the way I wished he would.

"I am breaking my own rules," he said. "The rules that I agreed to with the Fates. I am breaking them so that I can come here to warn you, daughter."

"Why?" I asked. "Why do you care? What made this your problem?"

His eyes flashed. "It is not your time to die. The gods still need you."

"No, they don't. Make new pawns," I snapped. "The world

doesn't obey you any longer. You are no more than myths and legends to the mortals. They don't need heroes anymore."

"They will always need heroes," he sighed.

The air continued to crackle with tension, the hairs standing up on my arms. The two of us stared at each other for a couple of moments, before he finally let out a grumble.

"I can see that I will not be able to stop you," he said.

"No," I said. "You won't."

"In that case I wish you luck. I will ask Hades to be kind to your souls."

I pressed my lips into a thin line. "Thank you. Before you go, can you answer one question."

"Ask."

"Who is behind this?"

"I cannot say."

"Is it truly Clotho?"

"No." His expression became grim. "I must go, but I will say this. Some gods have gained power from how this world has changed. Others have grown weaker. Our children are what is left of the old power. If you can survive, it would be better for this world."

His words chilled me to the bone.

I blinked, and he was gone.

———

I stepped into the basement of one of my clubs. Eric had brought our captives there, chaining them until I decided what we would do with them.

I'd found the bull, found out that Orpheus was partially behind this, but other than that...

You look defeated.

I hated Zeus. His words carried with me, even if I didn't want them to.

Madeline stood outside the door. She was back in her human form, wearing another dress. Her heels gave her an extra 3 inches of height. She was holding a glass of champagne, standing there like there wasn't a room full of people we had captured behind her. She raised an eyebrow. "I tortured all of them. It was Orpheus all along."

"It's him, but it's also not," I sighed. "I got the same information. It sounds like he's being used. Someone else is behind everything."

She took a sip of her champagne. "Did you get him?"

I was still falling apart. I needed a release. I needed to do something, needed to either fuck or kill. "Leave," I snarled at my men. "I want you to leave for the next hour. Don't come back until then."

I stood there, waiting for them to leave. When they were gone, I blew out a breath.

"I let him live," I said. "He was not the one that started these attacks. He was hired. He now owes me his life."

"I take it that means that he didn't have the knife."

"Correct," I growled. He was lucky. "I suppose Orpheus has it. We've been played."

"No," she said. "Percy, we got more information. Now we can take this to the rest of them and use it against him. Or even blackmail him to find the truth. We got answers tonight."

"I'm disappointed I didn't get more."

She pressed her lips together, regarding me carefully. She tilted her head to the side.

"What else is wrong? Clearly, something is bothering you. I can feel it through the bond. What happened?"

Of course, she could feel that.

It startled me.

Even knowing that we had our mating bond and that she had known me for so long, I couldn't think of the last time someone had asked me something like that. Except for occasionally Diego, but he'd never been so blunt.

I felt a fresh wave of anger and hurt. The monsters behind the door had taken him from me.

"Percy," she whispered.

I told her about my father. By the time I finished telling her all the details, her lips were parted in surprise. "What the actual fuck?" she asked. "And I wonder what he meant by the gods losing power."

"I don't know. I don't care either." I was tired and needed to somehow let go.

She took a step closer, her hands sliding up to my face. I closed my eyes, but she made a *tsking* noise. "Don't look away from me, please."

I opened my eyes. We were still covered in blood, the blood of our enemies. At least that part gave me a sense of satisfaction.

"What do you need right now?" she whispered.

"I need to either kill them or fuck you."

"Then fuck me," she said. "I'm at your service, *Daddy*."

"If I fuck you right now, it won't be gentle. It won't be easy. I'll try to break you."

"Then break me," she said. "I can take it."

"What if I want to tie you up and humiliate you?" I whispered.

"Do it."

"What if I wanted to—"

"Shatter me. Break me. Force me to do whatever you want me to do, even if I don't want to. I belong to you, right? Isn't that what you want?"

I let out a low growl, grabbing her wrists and slamming her against the wall. The champagne glass hit the floor, breaking everywhere. Her breath hitched, her pupils expanding.

"If we do this, there's no turning back."

She swallowed hard. It was clear she was aroused. She bared her fangs, and I felt the mating mark throb on my neck. "Aren't we past turning back now?"

We were. We really fucking were.

"Remember, you asked for this."

CHAPTER 18

PAPERCUT

M adeline

She pulled the hood off my head and my mouth fell open.

After I'd told her to do what she wanted, she'd put a hood over my head and had made me change back into my monster form. Then, she made me wait. For the first time in my life, I'd willingly stayed put for someone.

This was what she had prepared while I'd sat there in the dark.

The monsters and humans we had taken were all chained to chairs, all set up in a row. The ones that had been hunting me. They all wore expressions of fear.

I wondered if it was from her or me.

My eyes were covered with shades, so they didn't turn to stone. They were deadly silent.

"What are you doing?" I asked.

"I brought them all so they can observe this," Percy said.

Her words shouldn't have excited me, but they did. I had expected us to go back to her home, or perhaps even mine.

Not for her to bring me back to this room.

"I wanted your enemies to hear the truth before they die," she said simply. "I wanted an audience for what I'm about to do, and who better to watch than those that will soon perish because of what they tried to do to you? I want the last thing they ever hear to be how much better you are than them."

Fuck.

I had known I'd pushed her, but I didn't realize how far she was going to go.

I could see it in her eyes that she wanted to break me. Her shoulders pulled back as she stepped in front of me, her gaze meeting mine. She wore a simple bun, her body still clothed in black. She was stunning, deadly, mine.

Even though there was an audience, their shocked moans and cries were drowned out by her.

In her slender hands, she held a black glass jar. The lid was gone, but I could not see what was inside. I watched nervously as she reached inside, her eyes never leaving mine.

"What is it?" I asked.

"You're not really in a position to be asking me questions, kitten," she purred softly.

The chains around my wrist clanked, my breasts jiggling as I yanked against them. She raised a brow, regarding me coldly.

"In front of them?" I asked.

"Yes," she said. "As a monster too. A beautiful, terrifying, powerful monster."

I shivered. She'd bound my wings and tail, ensuring that I was truly stuck.

I wasn't going anywhere. I knew this, but I still tried. I felt like a snake caught in a trap. Instead of being able to strike, I simply wanted to slip away.

But I couldn't.

Not with her.

"I told you I would push you," she said. "You asked for this. You asked me to break down the last parts of our walls. You asked me to shatter your illusions." She chuckled and reached into the jar, pulling out a small torn piece of paper.

It was a strip, words written on the front.

"You did this for me?" I asked.

"Yes."

I held her gaze for a moment.

We were mates. Slowly but surely, I had been giving her piece after piece of my heart. I felt that happening again this morning, another brick torn from the wall I trapped myself behind.

I asked for this.

I had sensed her desperate need for release, and I wanted her to use me. I wanted her to use me however she needed to.

I meant it when I said I was hers.

Every part of me.

"You are going to read this out loud," she said. "You are going to read it for me and then I am going to shove it into your mouth. I want the ink of every word I wrote to sink onto your venomous tongue."

Fuck.

Sweat dripped down my back. My shoulders burned, my body tensing. I felt the weight of the audiences' gazes, their confusion and fear. I hated them, but I hadn't expected them to be a witness to this.

She was right.

I asked for this.

I wanted this.

It was a sort of torture that made me feel helpless. Completely fucking helpless and humiliated. And behind the shame of standing naked in front of them, chained this way, there was power.

"Do you understand?"

"Yes," I said.

"Yes, what?"

"Yes, daddy."

"Good. Do you remember your safeword?"

"Yes, daddy."

"Do you understand that I love you?"

My heart squeezed.

She turned the piece of paper over, holding it up so that I could read.

"No," I whispered, my heart leaping in my chest. "Don't make me say that. Not here. Not in front of them."

I couldn't do that. I had expected her to do many things, but didn't realize just how much pain she planned on inflicting. Part of me wished she'd cane me, spank me—anything that wasn't *this*.

"Say it," she commanded, her brows drawing together.

Tears sprang to my eyes. I blinked them back.

"Please don't make me."

"You will read it," she snarled. "You will read it because I want you to read it. Because I am *telling* you to read it. You are mine, you do as I wish, and you will do this or you will be punished. What you want simply doesn't matter right now. Read the fucking paper."

I let out a soft groan, holding back the tears. I had agreed to this dynamic. I wanted the cruelty, the pain. Because behind every blow was a love that I had craved for centuries.

"*I am beautiful*," I whispered.

I could feel myself crumbling from even seeing the words.

"You are," she agreed softly.

I whimpered, wishing that she would stop. Wishing that she wouldn't do this. "Please don't do this."

My words were ignored.

That terrified me and thrilled me all at the same time.

I could feel the weight of the gazes in the room. They had hunted me, hurt her, and now they would be witness to me submitting entirely. She was stealing my power from me, all while gifting me with a strength that was even greater than before.

"Let's see what else the jar of truth says."

Percy reached inside again, pulling out another piece of paper. She turned it around, showing me the scrawled words.

"Percy," I whimpered.

"Incorrect," she snapped. "I am not *Percy* right now."

"Daddy," I cried. "Please."

"Read. It."

I felt a flash of anger. Of rage. Heat flushed through my body, my blood boiling.

"I am cunning."

"Open your mouth."

Fuck.

When I didn't immediately open my mouth, her hand darted up. She grabbed my jaw and squeezed hard enough that I whimpered. My lips parted, and she shoved the two pieces of paper in.

"Don't swallow," she said. "It'll take time for these words to sink in."

I pushed them to the side of my mouth when she let go, still glaring at her. I was tittering from anger that she would do this to me, to fear that whatever was written in that jar would break me.

Sticks and stones could break bones, but words of kindness from someone whose love I didn't deserve would ruin me.

She smiled, electricity crackling around her. All I could see was her and her power.

"Let's see," she hummed.

She reached in again, pulling out yet another piece of paper.

"Read it."

She turned it around, showing it to me. Forcing me to look. I felt my breath whoosh out of me, my heart beating faster.

Why is she hurting me? Why is she making me say these things?

Sweat dripped down my spine. I strained against the chains again, to no avail.

"*I am worthy.*" I forced myself to say them, but those words hurt more than anything else possibly could have.

The woman standing in front of me had flogged me, spanked me, fucked me. She had captured my enemies and had chained them down, forcing them to watch us. Perhaps I should have been more focused on them, but I could hardly care. I had let her do all sorts of things to me, and yet nothing compared to the pain that I felt as those words sliced through me.

I felt a tear roll down my cheek as she rolled up the piece of paper and shoved it into my mouth. She reached into the jar again, showing me the paper.

"I am stronger than them."

My entire body began to tremble.

"I think we all agree," she said.

She rolled a piece of paper up and shoved it into my mouth. Tears rolled down my cheeks as she reached into the jar again. How long would this go on? How many had she prepared for this?

"How long are we doing this?" I asked.

"Until you can no longer speak."

Every muscle in my body tensed. She let out a soft hum,

unrolling another piece of paper. She showed it to me and raised a brow.

Every word felt broken.

"The gods were wrong about me."

She shoved it in, continuing.

"I am loved."

"I am needed."

"I am respected."

I am cherished. People love me. People worship me. I am a hero. I am a beautiful creature. I am wanted. I am desirable. I deserve happiness. I deserve love.

By the time we got to the last phrase, I could barely move my mouth.

She stepped closer, her lips almost touching mine. Tears rolled down my cheeks and I couldn't help myself. A sob wracked my body. I could barely look her in the eyes. I felt a wave of shame washed through me.

How could she stand in front of me and look at me like this? How could she ever desire me?

All of these pent-up emotions and fears had been plaguing me for so long that it was hard to distinguish lies from the truth.

"I want you to know that I wrote every single one of these out," she whispered. "I could have kept going, but I decided that would be enough. Every single motherfucker in this room deserves to die for hurting you. They hunted you, hated you, wished to kill you. All of them know they will die tonight, knowing that they could have saved themselves if they hadn't been so foolish. Are you ready for the last one?"

"Yes," I whispered.

She held up the last piece of paper and I felt every single thing inside me break. It was as if a wall had suddenly been bulldozed down. Every single part of me breaking, snapping, falling apart.

"I am yours," I sobbed.

"You are mine," she whispered, her voice filled with so much love.

She pushed the last piece of paper into my mouth. She tossed the jar to the side, the glass shattering against the concrete. She grabbed my face, forcing my mouth shut. I moaned as all the paper mushed in my mouth. I could taste the ink and the bitterness of the compliments that she had forced me to say.

She made me look her in the eyes, even as my vision blurred with more tears.

"Do you taste that?" she whispered. "Do you taste how much I love you? Do you see what I see? How strong and beautiful and loved you are? How I would do anything in the world for you? How you belong to me?"

I nodded, shaking.

"Good," she whispered. "Are you ready to let go?"

I nodded again. She reached up to the chains and undid them. The moment I was free, I collapsed to the floor, spitting out all the paper at her feet. She kneeled down, stroking my back as I did so.

She waited until I finished, but I couldn't stand up. My muscles refused to work. Her fingers were gentle as she unbound my wings and tail.

"Why would you do this to me?" I asked.

I was a mess. I was as broken and empty as the shattered jar.

"Because I love you. I need you to know how much I love you. I need you to know that when this is over, I will be here for you. Forever and always."

"That you're my god," I whispered, thinking of our bet.

"Yes. That I am your god and you will trust in me."

Her voice was soft, her touch, even softer. She was so gentle. Despite the torture she had just put me through.

I drew in a shaky breath, still trembling. I drew in another breath, and then another, until I finally started to feel...

Me.

Oh.

I leaned back, staring at the paper, the compliments, the love that she had for me.

I closed my eyes for a moment, truly letting these words sink in. All the way to my bones, to my heart of stone.

"I am thankful to be yours," I whispered.

She kissed my cheek.

"Would you like me to kill them? And then we can go home and cuddle and fight the world together."

"Yes," I said. "I think that would be best. I need...you."

"And you always have me," she said.

She rose and turned, raising her hands. I watched in awe as her lightning bolt appeared. I turned away as she struck them, her lethal power ending them one by one.

She sighed once it was over. I looked up at her, still on the ground.

I would do anything for her, I realized.

I loved her.

I had yet to say those words to her. I had carefully been avoiding them, ignoring them anytime they almost tumbled out.

But I loved her.

I loved her so much that it hurt.

She leaned down and picked me up, cradling me in her arms. I shifted back into my human form to make it easier on her. I laid my head on her shoulder, sighing as she carried me to the door.

She carried me up the set of steps, leaving all the destruction behind. Neither one of us felt a shred of remorse.

There was this feeling that every moment might be our last one, knowing what the Minoan Bull had said. Knowing that Orpheus was behind this, but also was only another piece in the puzzle.

I wouldn't think about that until tomorrow.

She carried me down the hall, giving a curt nod to the men that waited there. "Take care of the bodies," she commanded. And that was all it took. Our job was done when it came to them.

The monsters hunting me were dead.

Now we just had to find out who was truly behind all of this.

And somehow get that knife.

But those things didn't matter right now. Because she was right.

She was my god.

And I would trust her to the very end.

CHAPTER 19

CHASE

P ercy

I wasn't done with her yet.

By the time we pulled up to my house, her lips were practically glued to my neck. I let out a soft groan as she sucked the mated mark, pleasure radiating between our bond.

Even after breaking her, I needed more.

I opened the door and picked her up, carrying her bridal style to the front door. I slammed it shut behind us, her legs wrapping around my hips as we kissed.

"I'm not going to make it upstairs," I growled.

"I don't care," she huffed. "I'm yours."

Her words went straight to my core. "Say it again," I rasped.

"I'm yours."

I wanted to hear it over and over. I backed her against the wall hard enough that one painting threatened to fall, but that only made her giggle. I fisted her hair, tugging tight as we kissed.

She moved her hips, her pussy hot against me. She was still naked, her nipples hardening in the cool air.

I sank my teeth in her neck again, unable to stop myself. I was ravenous, a caged animal that had broken free. She cried out, her manicured nails digging into my skin. I tasted her blood, drinking from her like a vampire.

"Percy," she gasped.

I smiled against her. I loved it when she said my name that way.

I was letting go completely tonight. I could feel a dark and feral part of me rising now that it had a taste of freedom.

Her feet hit the ground as I released her suddenly, startling her.

"What are you doing?" she asked, her eyes widening. Her diamond pupils were black in the shadows, moonlight falling in fragments through the house.

"Do you remember your safe word?" I checked.

"Yes, of course."

"Do you want me to stop?"

She studied me for a moment, taking me in. She shook her head. "I don't want this to end."

"Then run," I whispered.

Her skin flushed. She took a tentative step to the side, still watching me.

"Run, little rabbit." My voice was harsh, ominous. "I've already killed once tonight. What's it to me if I kill again?"

She took off running. I watched as she went, her ass jiggling as she darted out the front door and into the night.

I expected her to run upstairs, but this made the chase all the more fun.

Woods surrounded my house, far enough from anyone that they wouldn't hear her begging and screaming.

I gave her a couple of minutes. In the meantime, I stripped off my clothes. I kicked off my boots and socks. I would go after her naked, considering she already was, too.

She was a monster. She knew how to get away. She knew how to fight.

She had the head start.

I would still let her think I wouldn't catch her.

Our paths would always cross. No matter how far we ran from each other, history had proven that our destinies were intertwined.

She would never truly escape me.

I stepped out the front door. It was so cold my breath came out in puffs. It iced my lungs, my blood heating as I looked out into the darkness. Goosebumps raised over my bare skin, my nipples hardening as I mentally readied myself to hunt.

To chase.

To catch.

I took off running, following my instincts. Being a demigod had its perks, and tracking my mate into the woods, knowing she was already close was one of them.

The sound of branches cracking underfoot satisfied me. I was being loud, letting her know I was coming for her.

I could feel her apprehension through our bond. I huffed as I ran between the trees, skidding to a halt. I looked around, taking in the rustle of the leaves and the eerie quiet.

Thunder rumbled in the distance. I smiled, the atmosphere responding to my lust. Storms would find us soon.

The animals knew there were predators in the woods.

I took off running again, grinning as I saw a flash of scales in the moonlight. I heard the hiss of snakes, moving to the right.

Excitement rolled through me, knowing that she had taken her monster form. That she wasn't holding back.

Madeline moved out of the way right as I reached for her. My foot gave way in a pile of leaves and I hit the ground, letting out a low laugh as I caught myself.

I looked up as she moved through the trees, getting away.

This is fun.

I sprinted after her again, the two of us moving in a wild blur. She moved faster now that she was in her monster form, pushing me to the edge.

She escaped deeper into the darkness. I pursued her, my muscles pumping, lungs dragging in breaths as I chased.

I was catching up to her.

There was nothing more satisfying than knowing she could feel me getting closer.

She turned right as I tackled her to the ground, the two of us tumbling hard together. I growled as her tail wrapped around my body, but I still pinned her beneath me.

I grabbed her wrists and slammed them against the ground, our faces nearly touching. We were both panting, her tail constricting my legs and hips.

"Got you," I rasped. "Let me go."

"*Make me.*"

Fucking bitch. I growled as I rolled with her, feeling her hit the roots of a tree hard enough that her tail loosened for a moment. I turned her onto her stomach, wrestling with her as I slipped the crook of my arm around her neck, pulling hard enough her breath left her.

"Submit," I growled.

"Never," she choked out.

I was so fucking wet. Electricity burned in my fingertips, and she let out a squeal, her breaths quickening.

"Submit," I snarled.

"Fuck you. I hate you."

I smiled. "I bet you do, kitten."

She attempted to roll, but it worked in my favor. In a swift motion, I let her roll onto her back again, and sat on her face.

Her talons dug into my thighs, the two of us struggling against each other. The snakes hissed. I growled as pain flared, feeling her cut through my skin as I rubbed my pussy against her face.

She groaned against me, still fighting, but she was slowly losing. Slowly giving in.

We fought against each other, even with my cunt pressed down on her mouth. Her talons raked my skin, blood dripping as I ran my hand down her torso, slipping two fingers inside her slit.

She cried out, her voice muffled against me.

"You're so fucking wet," I huffed. "*Fuck.*"

I could feel her saying *stop* against my pussy, but I didn't care.

Until she said her safeword, none of this was going to end. I was going to take her, use her, fuck her.

I slipped another finger inside of her, watching as her muscles twitched. She was fighting her submission, fighting the pleasure threatening to weaken her.

She was wet and ready, able to take even more. I moved my hips, humping against her face. I laughed as I felt a snake biting my ass cheek.

She groaned against me, fighting harder. I lifted for a brief second, allowing her to drag in a breath before sitting back down on her face.

"Make me bleed, bitch, I don't care," I chuckled, slipping four fingers inside her now.

I might be able to fit my entire hand inside her.

I worked her cunt, amazed at how wet she was. She was

dripping, her muscles relaxing around me, her body quivering as she cried out.

Finally, I felt her tongue pressing against my cunt, pushing inside.

"That's right," I said, doing my best to keep how fucking good that felt out of my voice. "Lick me while I fist you."

She tensed at the word *fist*, but became even more aroused. I raised a brow as I worked her with my hand, stretching her pussy, readying her for more.

Her tongue worked me harder as I curled my hand into a fist, slowly working it inside of her. She gasped against me, moaning helplessly as she licked my pussy while she took my entire fist. Her muscles squeezed around me, constricting.

I moved my hand inside her, signing out the words...

This

pussy

belongs

to

me...

She cried out as I hit her G-spot on the word "me", an orgasm rolling through her. She shook as she came so hard, hot liquid squirted from her. I hummed in satisfaction, feeling her relax completely.

"Good girl," I whispered. "You squirted for me, beautiful."

I still worked my fist in and out, lifting my pussy to let her catch her breath for a moment.

"*Oh gods*," she rasped.

"Do you know what I said?"

"Yes," she whimpered. "*My pussy is yours.*"

"That's right. Now, make me come, kitten."

She pulled my pussy back down to her eager lips, pleasure rolling through me. I groaned, tipping my head back as she ate me out, her tongue working its magic.

"Fuck," I growled.

I slowly pulled my fist from her, my back arching as I suddenly came on her face. My orgasm made me see stars, my entire body tensing as it rolled through me.

I groaned as all the tension finally broke, all the pent up aggression and need letting go. I sighed, blinking as I came down from the high.

I slid off her face, falling back onto the ground. Both of us laid there for a few minutes, catching our breaths.

When I could finally think and speak again, I looked over at her, reaching for her hand. She took mine, meeting my gaze.

"Hi," I whispered.

I felt a flash of guilt. I'd pushed her hard tonight, more than I'd ever done with anyone before. I'd broken her before chasing her down and fucking her. What if I'd hurt her?

"Percy," she said. "What's wrong?"

"I'm worried I harmed you."

Her brows pulled together, and she shook her head. "No, no. What do you mean?"

"We did a lot. I pushed you really hard, broke you and made you sob. And then I hunted you down and forced you to..."

She shook her head again and tugged me closer, pressing her forehead to mine. "You're silly," she whispered. "I loved every moment of it. I wanted it. I wanted you to hurt me. I needed that, do you understand?"

I swallowed hard, nodding. I was having a hard time believing her.

"I have an idea," she whispered. "Let's go home, take a long hot shower, and then cuddle in bed together."

"That sounds good."

"I have a confession to make, too."

My stomach twisted. "What is it?"

She gave me a slow smile. "I love you."

My breath left me, tears springing to my eyes. There had been a part of me that had already known that she loved me, but hearing her say it was the validation I needed. "You do?"

"I do," she said. "I really fucking do. I love you so much, Percy."

"I love you too," I said, tears rolling down my cheeks.

"I know you do, you sap."

I chuckled as she wiped the tears away.

"My goodness, you're a mess," she teased. "I know you enjoyed what you did."

"Of course," I said. "I'm just..."

"Having a drop."

"Yeah," I sighed, finally relaxing. "It was intense."

"It was. And yet even though you made me absolutely sob, I feel...good."

"Well, give it a couple days," I said. "Scenes like this sometimes have repercussions. If I pushed you too far..."

"I am okay, Percy," she said. "I promise you. And if I'm not, do you really think I wouldn't tell you? You're talking to the woman who ordered new curtains for the entire house between us killing, dealing with everything, and fucking."

I blubbered out a laugh. "My curtains are fine!"

"You said I could redecorate."

I grinned now, rolling my eyes. "You're insufferable."

"Yes and you love it."

We laid there for a few more minutes before finally trekking back home. I locked the door behind us and followed her upstairs. She turned on the shower and shifted back into her human form, pulling me beneath the hot water.

We kissed, but every touch was gentle. Sweet. I melted against her, the hot water bleeding out any tension that was left.

Steam surrounded us, fogging the mirrors as we finished showering.

"I think I could sleep for days," I groaned, reaching for two fluffy towels.

She snorted as I wrapped one around her. "I'd say weeks if we had that sort of time."

I pulled my towel around me, pressing my lips together. "We're going to stop them. Tomorrow we can deal with Orpheus and everyone else. We'll get the knife and I'll stop whoever is behind this."

She nodded. "I know."

She didn't sound convinced.

We finished drying off and flopped into bed. I pulled her close to me, breathing in her scent.

Everything would work out. It had to.

"I love you," I whispered.

"I love you too. *Sleep.*"

My eyes were already closing, sleep finding me fast.

CHAPTER 20

DISCORDIA

M adeline

"And what do we have here? A creature in hiding," a teasing voice said.

I turned around, ready to kill whomever was standing behind me.

The moon was high, and I'd chosen this spot in the gardens, to hide, for a reason. No one came here at night, and I could typically steal some food from the kitchens. I'd grown tired of hunting. The mortals made bread and cheese and they were delicious. It was easier to take from them.

A woman stood with long black hair and a black cloak. Her lips looked as though she'd bitten into fresh cherries, bright red and gleaming.

"Go away," I snarled.

"I am here to ask for a favor. In return, I will give you a bit of my magic so that you can walk as a mortal. Wouldn't you like *your legs back, Medusa? I know you weren't born as a monster."*

My heart skipped a beat. Her words were convincing enough that I might indulge her. "Who are you?"

"Eris. Discordia. I have many names."

"No," I said immediately. "I don't speak to the gods or goddesses."

"I can help you, Medusa. Then you can be whoever you want to be."

I shook my head; the snakes hissing. I hated the gods. I hated them all. And I hated that their precious demigod children got to walk while monsters were stuck in the shadows.

"It's an easy favor. The spell would last twenty years, and then you'd owe me another favor."

"I'm not a fan of favors."

"I think that you'll find you enjoy what I give you in return."

———

I sat up abruptly in bed, sweat covering me. My heart hammered in my chest, every muscle in my body tense. The memory lingered in my mind, poignant enough that I could almost smell the flowers that had grown in those gardens.

Our bedroom was dark. Percy snored next to me, still deeply asleep.

What the fuck?

I could feel pieces of the puzzle finally sliding into place. The monsters, the drachmas, the ancient cards.

I should have known.

I trembled as I carefully slid out of bed and grabbed a robe, pulling it on. I snatched my phone off the dresser, checking my messages. Aside from the usual ones from Ella, everything else was quiet.

I half expected there to be an ominous email from the goddess.

We all had our secrets. I had plenty. Prior to being part of the Three Fates Mafia, the only way I could exist in the mortal world was by doing favors for a goddess. One that approached me long ago to do her dirty work.

There were reasons I hated them. She'd proven again I could never trust one of them.

I hadn't always been a monster. It was a brief moment in time, a blink really, where I had been a mortal woman. One that was beautiful, that served the goddesses in their temples.

That hadn't lasted long. One god had taken me against my will, and a jealous goddess had turned me into *Medusa*. I'd been a victim and then punished for it. History always punished women for the sins of man. How the Fates could allow them to do the things they did was the very reason I never fully trusted them.

The gorgons had taken me in, even though I wasn't born of them. I went from being a beautiful and beloved woman to a feared and forsaken monster.

I'd never learned how to truly embrace myself. Only Percy had shown me bit by bit that I was still *me*.

The woman that had tried to cut off her own tail off ages ago thanked the woman I was now for healing.

I was silent as I left the room, carefully closing the door behind me. I felt sick as I thought about the past.

The words Percy had forced me to say came back to me as I went downstairs.

I am strong. I am beautiful. I am worthy.

The kitchen was quiet. I went to the stack of unopened packages on the counter, going through her mail. I scowled as I found the unlabeled box, my stomach doing somersaults as I peeled back the tape.

I opened the box and looked inside, fear icing in my veins.

Inside, there was nothing but a severed hand. I knew that hand. I knew the manicured nails at the end, and the golden threads that lay lifeless against the cardboard.

Discordia had sent Percy the hand of a Fate.

I had a feeling that the box in my abandoned apartment held the other.

I wrinkled my nose and reached inside, gripping it. I gasped as the fingers interlaced with mine. I gagged, shaking as hard as I could until the bitch finally let go. It dropped inside the box. The fingers twitched.

"Disgusting," I snarled.

Behind the disgust was the realization. I could almost hear the click as pieces fell into place.

It hadn't been Clotho that had brought Percy that letter.

It wasn't the Fates that had constructed the elaborate ploy to fuck with her and me.

Nor had they plotted my death.

Discordia, Eris, daughter of Nix, goddess of manipulation, chaos, my *ex-boss*—was an evil, wretched cunt.

Zeus had told Percy that others had gained power as this world had changed. He had been truthful.

I swallowed hard, staring at the hand. Had she killed the Fates?

The thought chilled me to my core.

Without the Fates, I wasn't sure what would happen to our world. My life thread certainly wasn't the only one that would end.

I needed to get the other box. I made a gagging noise and went to the kitchen sink, washing my hands quickly before grabbing my phone. At least the severed hand didn't smell like it was rotting. That would have pissed me off more than anything.

I opened the screen, hitting the call button. It rang a couple times, and then my very groggy assistant answered.

"Hello?"

"Hi, Ella. I need you to do something for me," I said. I tapped my fingernails on the counter, rolling my eyes as she yawned.

"It's 3 A.M., Madeline."

"Yes, and I pay you very well. I need you to get something from my apartment."

"Where the guy *died?*"

"Yes. That one. I need the box that came in without a label last week."

Ella groaned again. "It's the middle of the night and I had a lot to drink before bed and I—"

"You have an hour or you're fired." I hung up before she could protest, and then it occurred to me I didn't tell her where to bring it. "For fuck's sake," I muttered to myself.

I texted her the address and then released a heavy breath. My shoulders still wouldn't relax, even on the exhale.

The drachmas, the cards, the hands, the stabbing. And of course, the Minoan Bull had been offered something he couldn't resist.

I knew what it felt like to be in that position.

Over the centuries, I had done many things. But almost every '*bad*' thing had been for someone else. It had earned me a reputation, one that I quite enjoyed despite my distaste for actually getting my hands dirty.

Before the Fates had made their offer for the Three Fates Mafia, doing favors for the goddess of chaos had been my bread and butter. A favor every twenty years to walk with legs again was an easy price to pay, even if it meant killing someone.

For a long time, I had been grateful to her.

Percy did not know that the only time I'd ever betrayed the goddess was in order to save her.

I let the memories come, even though they hurt. There had been a train ride years ago, one of the many times my path had crossed with hers. I'd just received the letter from the Three Fates Mafia, but hadn't told Discordia I would no longer be working for her.

In the cosmic order of things, even the Fates trumped the gods and goddesses. At least, that was how it used to be.

Discordia had wanted me to kill the passenger in the Pullman private cart on the 1 P.M. train to London. The moment I stepped onto the cart, I knew it was Percy that was waiting.

Her scent had never changed over the years. Even now, she reminded me of the wild waves and stormy skies. She was a breath of fresh air in a world that wished to suffocate me.

That's when I had decided I couldn't work with Discordia.

I would accept the Fates offer.

Then I'd asked her to join too.

I'll never forget.

I squeezed my eyes shut, thinking of the last time I saw the goddess.

"Did you take care of the favor?"

Discordia sat in a velvet chair behind a massive desk in her beautiful home. There had been a time I would have been envious of her, but my own properties were just as magnificent.

Loose dark hair curled down her back. She wore a sky blue afternoon dress with a royal blue neckline, one that dipped far too low for what current society deemed acceptable. I had always admired her lack of caring, despite trying to blend in with the mortal world herself.

Unlike the other gods and goddesses, she seemed to prefer

walking amongst mortals. But, being the goddess of chaos and disorder, I was certain that was how she entertained herself.

I shifted in my seat, not sure how to answer her question.

This conversation would not be pleasant, but it was best I was honest.

"I must discuss that with you," I said, forcing a pleasant smile. "That particular favor."

She was writing on a piece of paper, scrolling in blood red ink. I was certain it more than likely was blood.

"Then speak."

"I did not kill the passenger. You knew that I wouldn't."

The pen paused, ink pooling on the paper in an uncomfortable silence. She let out an unsatisfied hum. "Well, that is a disappointment. You knew what I expected of you and you know the consequences of failing to complete the task I require. I suppose you will just have to go back to living in the world as a monster again."

"About that. The Fates have come to me with a proposition, and who am I to decline them? I can no longer work for you, Discordia."

She was silent again. I bit the inside of my cheek as I waited for her to reply. She let out another soft hum, and then slowly put her ink pen down. She looked up at me, her eyes burning into my very soul. A shiver worked down my spine.

"You can tell the Fates no, can't you, dear?"

"I cannot," I said.

I had to stay strong. I could survive this. I'd already come this far.

The things that I had done...

Suddenly, the goddess was standing right in front of me. Darkness saturated the room, the sunlight choked out by black smoke. I fell back against my chair, fear curling through me.

"You can't expect to tell a goddess no without repercussions," she hissed. "How dare you? After everything I've done for you."

"Everything you have done for me has been a debt paid. I betrayed people for you. Lied for you. Killed for you."

She glowered, her eyes burning.

"The Fates chose me," I protested. "I didn't ask for this. They chose me."

The darkness receded, the room slowly returning to normal despite the chill I felt.

"Leave," she snarled. "Get out of my sight. Never ask me for another thing."

I stood up and readied to leave, but her hand darted out. I yelped as she tore off the necklace I wore, breaking the chain. The moment the jewel was taken from me, my body began to change into that of a monster.

"Give that back!" I yelled.

"This was my gift to you," she snapped. "You don't deserve it anymore. Have fun getting wherever you need to go looking like that. I'll never forget what happened here."

A knock startled me, pulling me from my daze. My heart was still hammering, my blood rushing as I left the kitchen, grabbing a set of sunglasses and putting them on.

I tiptoed to the front door, annoyed by how cold the hardwoods were. She needed more rugs in her house. Or heated flooring.

I added those two things to my mental checklist as I peered through the peephole.

Ella stood on the other side, holding a box. She was wearing pajamas, her hair pulled back in a messy bun. This was the first time I'd ever seen her without makeup.

I pulled open the door. "The circles under your eyes are ghastly."

She sighed as she handed me the box. "It's past 3 A.M. and someone woke me from my beauty sleep."

I made a face at her. "You need more than sleep for those. A spa day and some sort of ice facial."

"Okay, okay. Point made. You look exhausted too."

I snorted. "I'm positive that even when I'm exhausted, I still look exquisite."

Ella smiled. "For your demigod?"

I cocked my head. I realized I didn't really like Percy being referred to that way. "My girlfriend. You're free to go now."

"You're welcome, by the way."

"Yes, yes, thanks for doing the job I pay you very well for. You've practically been on vacation for the last two weeks. Was there anything else weird?"

"No, except for the fact that you never tell me what's happening anymore," she whined. "I can help with whatever is going on."

I snatched the box from her. "You absolutely cannot help with anything. In fact, you'd just be in the way. Go home, Ella. I appreciate you grabbing this for me. If I need anything else, I'll call."

"Are you sure I can't help? I can bring you your coffee. I never forget."

"Ella," I hissed. "Go away."

Her expression became mopey as I slammed the front door. I carried the box to the kitchen, annoyed now. Maybe I'd find a new assistant after all of this was done. She'd been so whiny recently and I didn't like whiny mortals. They reminded me of mewling kittens, except they were ugly and annoying.

I sat the box on the counter and opened it, grimacing as my suspicions were confirmed. This box held Clotho's left hand, the other held the right.

The Clotho that had talked to Percy was more than likely a disguised Discordia.

Creating chaos was her greatest strength.

The monsters, the drachmas, the favors. All of it made sense. My past had come back to haunt me.

I should have known that she wouldn't let any of this go.

The day that I had quit working for her was the last time I'd seen her. That had been about a century ago.

A lot could change in a century.

Even with the time that had passed, she intended to make me suffer for snubbing her. It was petty and bitchy, but when you were a being like *her*, you had to get your rocks off somehow.

This entire time, we'd been trying to stop *me* from dying. But now, all I could think of was how it was Percy that needed protecting.

Not me.

I heard movement upstairs. I cursed under my breath and moved the boxes quickly, shoving them into an empty cabinet. My back straightened right as Percy came into the kitchen, her lightning bolt drawn and hissing.

"Mads, what the fuck?" she hissed, putting her bolt away. She flipped on the kitchen light, which made me blink rapidly as my vision adjusted.

"Sorry," I said, waving my hand. "Turn off that fucking light. Gods, do you have fluorescents in here? I'm changing those too." She flipped it off, raising a brow. "I needed some water. But I don't know where you keep the cups."

She stared for a moment, clearly still half asleep. "Right, right. Sorry, kitten. I never got us water before we fell asleep."

"It's okay," I said. "I'm sorry I woke you, darling."

I stepped in front of the cabinet hiding the hands as she opened another, pulling out two glasses. She poured us each a glass of water and then came to me. I took it from her, raising a brow.

She narrowed her gaze. "Drink it up and then come back to bed. And next time, just turn on the kitchen light."

"I can see fine in the dark," I said. "There's moonlight."

She made a face and drained her cup. She waited for me to do the same and then went back upstairs.

I glanced at the cabinet and then followed her.

I didn't like withholding information from her, but the less she knew about Discordia the better.

I would need to face this alone. The thought of Percy being harmed because of someone I used to work for was something I couldn't handle.

Tomorrow morning, I'd sneak away and deal with things. I'd let Percy go after Orpheus and confront the goddess of chaos.

One way or another, I would keep my mate safe.

CHAPTER 21

A DAY OFF

P ercy

I poured a glass of orange juice as I messaged everyone in the Three Fates Mafia.

Except for Theseus and Orpheus.

It was a simple email, one that included the Fates as well, and I felt both pride and anger as I hit the send button.

```
Attention,

I have found Orpheus guilty of attempting to
murder Madeline aka Medusa. This is treason
    that will not be taken lightly. Do not
interfere with his punishment and/or death.

        Not So Best Wishes,
           Perseus
```

Madeline came into the dining room, sitting down next to me.

"Virgin mimosa?" I offered.

She laughed as she stole a fresh biscuit from the pile between us. Eric had visited early this morning and had cooked for us, which had been kind. It was something that Diego did before he was murdered.

Now that I had got some sleep, some sex, and some food, I felt like a well-balanced person again. I knew what I had to do. I knew what I could handle. And I had my power under control.

Madeline poured herself a cup of coffee and a glass of orange juice. "What's our plan for the day?"

"Confronting Orpheus," I said.

"Hmm."

I raised a brow as I sipped my orange juice. "No?"

"What if we take a day off and let things settle?"

I simply stared at her. I wasn't sure what her reasoning was for suggesting that. The two of us were fighting against time, and we were approaching the eleventh hour.

"We can't," I said. "We can rest once this is all over. We have to get Orpheus, get the knife, and go after the true enemy."

She let out a soft breath, taking a sip of her coffee. I raised a brow.

"Do you disagree?" I pressed.

"Yes. I think we should take the day off."

"Why?"

"I already said why."

"Yes, but what's the real reason?"

She scoffed, taking up her mug. "Well, now I'm offended."

She was being ridiculous. I had known her long enough to know when she wasn't being forthright, and this was a perfect example of one of those times.

Not to mention, I could feel her unease through our mated bond.

"Madeline," I said pleasantly. "Tell me why."

"I want to spend the day with you. Maybe after last night, I just want a day off to read books and hang out."

"Madeline. You and I both know you do not spend your time reading books. You spend your time shopping, painting, sculpting."

"I listen to audiobooks. That counts."

I blinked. "That does, but that's not my point."

"We've done nothing but work. We've done nothing but fight. I just want to be us. No drama, no problems. And then tomorrow, we can go back to being bad ass mafia women who have to rule the world."

"Kitten, part of being bad ass mafia women that have to rule the world is that we don't get days off from being that. Besides, I sent an email."

"I saw. Might as well keep everyone on their toes." She leaned forward, the morning light gleaming in her beautiful eyes. She was truly gorgeous. A distraction. I could almost feel every sane thought flying out the window. "Come on," she purred. "Don't you want to spend the day in bed together?"

I sighed in frustration. "Of course I do. But—"

"Here's another thought. What if we don't win? What if we lose? Wouldn't you be happier knowing we had at least one day like this? One with no trouble?" Her voice was pleading, almost a beg.

For fuck's sake. How could I say no to that? I shook my head, leaning back in my chair.

"Seriously?" I asked. "Is that really what you want?"

"Yes." She grinned, knowing she'd already won.

I was a sap and a sucker.

"Fine. But if something happens today, we have to act."

"Of course," she purred, standing up. She came around and slid her arms around my neck, resting her chin on my shoulder. "Are we alone, or are some of your men running around?"

"We're alone," I said, my mouth going dry.

"Oh excellent. Why are you wearing so many clothes, darling?"

Fuck. I couldn't protest now. My heart beat a little faster as she pulled my blouse up and unlatched my bra, baring me quickly. My head fell back on a groan as she teased my breasts.

"You're insatiable," I rasped.

"I am with you. Come upstairs for breakfast."

She left me sitting completely stunned.

I blew out a breath and pushed the chair back, standing. I heard Madeline's soft giggle, the stairs to our bedroom creaking.

This was the life I'd always wanted with her. Chasing her upstairs to our room where we would spend hours feasting on each other, loving each other.

I pulled off my pants, kicking them to the side. I didn't care that I was leaving breakfast on the table. I had a meal waiting for me upstairs.

I walked through the house, following her up the steps. I went to my bedroom and pushed open the door. She wasn't in here, I realized.

"Oh," I chuckled. She had gone to the kink room. Of course.

I went to the other room and pushed open the door, leaning against the doorway. I gripped the top of the frame, blowing out a breath of surprise.

Madeline was spread out on one of the S sofas, her legs already parted and body completely naked. She'd pulled back the curtains and natural sunlight poured into the room, high-lighting every toy and object of pleasure I had here.

"You really want to tease me, don't you?" I asked.

"Always," she said.

Her fangs glistened as she shifted right before me. My grip tightened on the top of the door frame as she slid her fingers down to her pussy, her tail draped over the end of the couch. Her wings spread behind her, the tips catching the sun. I could see the veins through her skin, her scales glittering like crushed jewels.

"Make yourself come for me," I demanded, my words harsh.

I stayed in the doorway as I watched her, letting out a soft moan as she continued to please herself.

Fuck. She was driving me crazy. Today wasn't going how I expected, but I couldn't complain. Not when I had her in front of me like this. My grip on the doorway tightened enough that I could hear the wood cracking as I watched.

"Are you just going to watch?" she teased.

"Until you beg me to come touch you, yes."

She blushed, her breath hitching as she kept touching herself.

"Are you wet for me?" I asked, dropping my voice lower, softer.

She whimpered. "Please."

I gave her a knowing smile. "Really? You'll have to do better than that."

She slipped a finger inside herself, stroking her cunt for me. In and out, over and over again. I bit my lower lip as I watched, the two of us having a standoff. She was trying to wait me out, to see if I would go to her.

She was cute for thinking that I would give in to her so easily. Did I want her? Yes, more than anything. But what I wanted more than that was to hear her beg for me to fuck her.

She cursed, her eyes blazing. "Come to me," she said.

"Beg me," I countered. "You know you won't win, so be a good girl and beg me to."

She was being a brat. I gave her a simple smile, holding my expression as I watched. She bit back another curse, arching against the sofa.

I left the doorway and enjoyed the way her eyes lit up as she believed I was going to her. Instead, I moved to the armoire, opening it up and turning my back to her. Ignoring her even as she touched herself.

She groaned in frustration.

"This isn't fair," she cried.

I held back a laugh, still ignoring her. She knew what I wanted. Being a brat wasn't the way to get it. It wouldn't take her long to figure that out.

I hummed to myself as I looked through the cabinet, deciding what I was going to use on her. She called my name, but I ignored her, torn between a monster dildo and a vibrator.

"Fine," she growled. "Please. Please come fuck me, daddy. I want you to touch me more than anything else."

The words were fine, but her voice still dripped with a hint of sass.

I looked over my shoulder and simply raised an eyebrow.

She rolled her eyes dramatically, throwing her hands up.

"I don't know why you're being so disobedient," I said. I didn't drop my condescending tone. "If you were being obedient, perhaps you would be rewarded. I don't like it when you behave like this. You're not a brat," I said. "So stop acting like one."

"Maybe I am a brat."

Oh. So she was deciding she was going to be difficult.

Instead of picking up the vibrator as I had planned, I chose a leather paddle that had the words 'dirty whore' on it. They were made of metal, the edges sharp enough that they would sting.

I turned around. "I want you to morph back into your human form and bend over."

"What if I don't want to?"

"Then I will tie you to the bed with a vibrator on your cunt and leave for the rest of the day."

She smirked.

Now she was pissing me off.

I marched to her and grabbed a fistful of writhing serpents, yanking her head back.

"Shift. Now."

"I thought you liked my monster form."

"Do I?" I asked. "Maybe. But you know what I like more?"

"What?"

"A compliant sub. Bend the fuck over, Mads, or there will be consequences."

She glared at me as I released her, but her body was already shifting back to human. The moment she had legs, I grabbed her and twisted her around.

She kicked out at me.

"I don't know why you're making things so hard on yourself," I said.

"Maybe I want you to be rough."

"Did you know there's such a thing as asking? Did you know that maybe if you would've said hey, I want you to be rough with me, I might have said yes? Instead, you chose to be a bratty little bitch."

I dragged her off the sofa and put her on her knees, bending her over the lowest curve. She wiggled against me, but stopped the moment she felt the paddle against her ass.

"We're supposed to be fighting people, and now you're going to do so with a sore ass," I said. "Remember me when our enemies think you're walking funny."

"I'll just turn them to stone."

I brought the paddle down hard. Harder than I'd normally start out with, but that was the point. She gasped as I pulled it away, red welts already forming.

Thank the gods I'd bolted the furniture down.

I didn't give her a moment to recover. Instead, I brought the paddle down again. She cried out, the sound of the leather against her skin echoing through the room. I smacked her again and again, pushing her to the edge almost immediately.

Every time I pulled the paddle back, the phrase 'dirty whore' was imprinted in her skin.

She groaned, her nails digging into the fabric. She gripped the edge of the sofa as I spanked her again. Her ass was red, and some of the places where the words had hit were breaking.

"You're going to make me bleed," she rasped.

"And? I'll blood-bond every single toy that I own. It's not like I'm going to ever play with someone else. Who cares if your blood is all over everything that I own in this fucking room?"

A shiver went through her. I knew she was wet. It didn't matter that every single strike was hurting her more and more, she wanted the pain.

What if she came from me spanking her ass?

She yelped as I continued. I kept speaking to her, finding a rhythm that was similar to what it would be like if I were fucking her right now. Over and over again, I smacked her ass cheeks, watching as she began to writhe and groan.

"Is this what you wanted?" I taunted. "Is this how you wanted me to take you?"

"Yes," she moaned. "Yes, yes, yes."

I chuckled as I continued to hit her. Her skin was blood red now. Crimson dripped from a fresh cut.

"I'm going to come," she rasped. "Fuck."

But I would not let her. As soon as she said that, I pulled

back the paddle. I stood up, leaving her kneeling there. She scoffed, clearly bewildered.

"What are you doing? Why did you stop?"

"Did you really think I was going to let you come? You still haven't begged me. And until you beg, you will not get what you want."

"Fuck you," she growled.

"And you still have your attitude. Fine. Fuck around and find out."

It turned out that I would use the dildo. I went to the cabinet and stripped off my underwear, replacing them with a harness. I took the dildo out of the cabinet, along with the rope.

Madeline started to turn over as I went back to her. I grabbed her by her hair and hauled her up, enjoying the way she squealed.

"You can't make me do anything," she hissed.

And yet I could hear the tremble in her voice.

"I can and will," I said.

I dragged her over to the Saint Andrew's cross. Her eyes widened as I pushed her against the wood, tying her wrists quickly. I tightened them until her arms were above her head.

"You can be a monster again," I said.

"What if I don't want to?"

I put the dildo right in front of her face, holding it there. "Do you want this going in dry?"

Her eyes flickered, her lips pressing together. She said nothing, but she shifted back to her monster, back to the form I loved. Her tail wrapped around the base of the cross.

"Suck it," I commanded. "Get it ready for yourself. If you don't get it wet, it's still going inside of you."

She muttered something under her breath and then started to suck it. I watched as she began with the tip, using her saliva to wet the entire toy. I held it for her as she did so, and then used my other hand to caress her body.

Her pussy was dripping. I ran my thumb over her clit, teasing her slowly.

She sucked in a breath, a helpless moan leaving her.

"Keep working that cock," I said.

"*Fuck me,*" she moaned, sucking more.

"Does your ass still ache even though you're a monster now?" I asked.

She nodded as she bobbed her head up, and down, her eyes flickering with heat.

"Good," I said. "I'll reward you for finally listening to me."

I pushed two fingers inside of her and she moaned, her eyes fluttering as she kept sucking. I eased them in and out, tormenting her.

She trembled, her muscles tensing. I could feel her pleasure through our bonds, and so I stopped.

I pulled the dildo away.

"Please," she groaned. "Please don't stop. I'm so close. I'm so fucking close."

"There we go," I whispered, leaning in. Our lips almost touching, her words still tumbling out.

"Please. Please. I need to."

"I know," I said. "And I'll let you, now that you're being so good for me."

I took the toy and fit it into my harness, enjoying her constant pleas. Between her saliva and how wet she already was, this thing would slide in with ease.

I held the tip against her cunt and slowly thrust forward. Her head fell back, sweat beading along her forehead. I slid my hand around her neck as I gave her every single inch, squeezing the sides as my hips pressed to hers.

"Fuck," she moaned. "You feel so good."

"So do you," I whispered, releasing her neck and kissing where my mark was.

She gasped, her hips moving against mine. I pulled back and then filled her again. Her tail wrapped around me, holding the two of us close as I fucked her. I groaned as I felt the very tip of her tail rub my pussy.

"I'll take you," I rasped.

She whimpered and thrust her tail up, filling me with it. We cried out together. All the tension melted into full intimacy, my arms wrapping around her as I took her.

I hadn't realized that I was already at the edge too. I kept fucking her, every thrust deep and rhythmic. Her tail did the same, filling me over and over again. Waves of pleasure had me careening. Our lips met in a hot kiss, our whimpers melting into each other.

"I'm going to," she moaned. "Please let me."

"Come for me. I'll come with you."

I watched in a haze as she stiffened, her head falling back in orgasmic bliss. I followed suit. Her tail thrust into me again right as I came. Seeing her come sent me into a state of absolute lust.

She fell against me, her arms still tugging against the ropes. We held onto each other, my head resting on her shoulder. I was still buried inside of her, her tail still binding us, the tip still inside of me.

"I love you," she sighed happily.

"I love you too," I said. "Even when you're a brat."

"You love me because I can be a brat," she chuckled.

True. I did love that about her.

I slowly pulled out and groaned as her tail pulled free, slick with my come.

I reached up and unbound her from the ropes. The two of us gravitated towards the rug in the middle of the room, lying on the floor together. I closed my eyes, enjoying the rays of sunlight on us.

"Okay. You were right," I finally said. "This was a good idea."

"Taking the day off?"

"Yes."

She propped herself up, giving me a snarky smile. "Told you."

I nodded. "Even though I'm sure a million things are going wrong, as we speak."

"None of that matters. Not right now, anyway." She sat up more, glancing at the doorway. "I'm going to get us water."

"I'll come with you," I said, sitting up.

"No, no. Just stay," she said. "I'd like to get you water."

I stared at her for a moment and then laid back down. "Fine," I mumbled. "If you insist."

She nodded and rose, leaving the room and heading downstairs. I sighed and closed my eyes, basking in the warm glow of being with her.

Within a couple minutes, she came back with our glasses. "I added strawberry flavoring," she said.

I made a face, but took it. She settled back down next to me, the two of us draining our cups. The flavoring tasted strange, but I wouldn't fight her on it.

"We could go cuddle," she suggested.

"I thought you wanted to read books."

"Books and cuddles."

I yawned and nodded. "Okay. Bed sounds good. This session wiped me out."

"I'm sure it did."

Maybe it would be cuddles and books for her, and a nap for me instead.

CHAPTER 22

CYCLOPS

M adeline

I didn't like manipulating the woman I loved, but it was necessary to keep her safe.

It hadn't even been ten minutes after drinking the glass of water that she'd passed out.

I didn't like drugging her, but that was also necessary to keep her asleep long enough. Long enough for me to confront the goddess and get everything worked out.

She hadn't even questioned the flavoring. I knew that shit didn't taste like strawberry, but she trusted me, she would never second guess what I said.

My heart ached.

I got dressed quickly, threw on shades, and grabbed the bag that I had prepared before I had distracted her earlier.

I took one last look at her, drinking her in. She was curled up in bed, her left foot hanging out of the blankets. She snored softly, her expression serene.

"I'm sorry," I whispered. "It's for you. I'm doing this for you."

I went downstairs with my bag, wincing at the ache I felt in my ass cheeks. My ass needed a massage and kisses, not to be out fighting a goddess.

Remember me when your enemies think you're walking funny.

Well, I would.

I double checked the contents, seeing that the hands of Fate were there, along with my weapons. I'd wrapped the hands in plastic, which was still disgusting, and sometimes the fingers would flinch.

I imagined Clotho was still alive somewhere.

I just wasn't sure where.

I checked every knife and gun. Two of the guns I'd taken were Percy's and seemed to be specifically designed for monsters.

I wasn't even sure that I would need them. I was strong and fast. But weapons were useful, regardless.

My shoulders were tense, my muscles coiled up. I forced myself to take three deep breaths.

One.

Two.

Three.

Guilt. Guilt and worry. I tried to push the emotions aside, but it was impossible when I knew what I was doing would hurt her. But she would understand once everything was worked out.

If it didn't work out, at least we'd had the day together.

I slung the bag over my shoulder and then paused, biting my lower lip.

I'd at least leave her a note. One that would send her in a different direction.

Going back to the kitchen, I fished around in the drawers until I found a notepad and a pen.

HELLO DARLING,

I KNOW YOU WILL PANIC WHEN YOU WAKE UP AND I'M GONE. I'M SORRY FOR THAT. BUT DON'T WORRY, FOR ONCE I AM GOING TO BE THE HERO. TRUST ME, I CAN DO THIS. GO AFTER ORPHEUS IN THE MEANTIME.

WITH LOVE,
MADS

That should suffice. I exhaled slowly, put it on the counter, and then left the house.

The sun was setting, reflecting in the windows as I went to the car in the drive. Her driveway was empty aside from the two guards standing there. I didn't recognize either.

"Miss?" one asked. "May I drive you somewhere?"

"I'm running an errand for your Mistress," I said. "Let me have the keys."

He hesitated.

"Give. Them. To me."

He tossed them to me immediately and then stepped off to the side, out of the way.

"I shall return," I lied. Well, hopefully it wasn't a lie.

Hopefully, I would return.

I pressed the unlock button and then tossed my bag into the backseat. I went around to the driver's side and slid in, turning on the car and revving the engine.

My plan was to go back to my apartment and summon the

goddess. In the past, the best way to reach her was to do exactly that. A little bit of blood, a little bit of prayer, and in theory, she would appear right there.

I hoped.

This entire plan was riding on a lot of hope.

If the goddess appeared, then...

Well, I wasn't sure.

I'd either shoot her or ask for a bargain. The gods always liked bargains.

I pulled out of the driveway, speeding far away from Percy's home. From our home. I watched as it grew small in the rearview mirror.

Maybe I'd be back home before she woke up.

I cranked up the radio as I drove, trying to drown out my thoughts. It was easier if I just went into autopilot mode instead of over thinking everything right now.

I was certain that she was expecting me. She would've known that the moment I saw the boxes, I would remember her. Perhaps the reason I had had that memory or dream was because she had sent it to me.

It was hard to say, but she knew me and I knew her as well as anyone could know a goddess.

She would be ready for me. The problem was, I wasn't sure how I was going to convince her to leave us alone. Or to at least leave Percy alone. And to give the Fates their hands back.

Fear rarely plagued me, but right now I could feel it all the way to my bones. That she had maimed a Fate was troubling. And where were the others? Why weren't they interfering? Or was this their plan all along?

That was the problem when thinking about fate. Destiny.

The idea that someone had already written my ending for me infuriated me. The idea that they already knew where my path would go pissed me off. I liked to think that they didn't really know, and were more there to help guide us along. But who was I to know the truth?

I gripped the steering wheel as I raced down the highway. As I drove into the heart of Moirai the streets became more crowded, the buildings taller.

I ignored several stoplights, risking the lives of mortals and not giving a shit. I wasn't in the mood.

Within what felt like the blink of an eye, I was pulling into my apartment building's parking garage.

I found the perfect spot and twisted around in my seat to grab my bag. I snatched it and got out of the car, slamming the door shut a little too hard.

I stood there for a moment, taking in my surroundings, realizing how strangely silent the garage was.

It smelled strange too.

My lips pressed together. I pulled the bag around, unzipping it quickly and pulling out one of Percy's guns. A bullet wouldn't be useful on a goddess, but who knew what else was in the garage. Especially with how she kept hiring all of these monsters.

Everyone loved her favors. Everyone loved to serve her and be the recipients of her chaos. I had been one of them for so long.

Not anymore.

Never again.

I shouldn't have forgotten about her. I shouldn't have believed that she would simply let me go. That's how they were. The gods never forgot if someone pissed them off.

I cocked the gun as I began my walk towards the elevator doors. Now that the sun was setting, it was cold outside, especially here. I breathed in the scent of gasoline and something else, something I couldn't quite place.

Something not human nor demigod.

"I'm really sick of all the shit that's happened," I muttered.

I just wanted to live in a beautiful house with my demigod wife, fuck all day, and be merry. Was that too much to ask for?

A shadow moved to my left, and I spun. Three colossal figures emerged, each appearing like a man but with one eye at the center of their heads.

Cyclopes.

Not only Cyclopes, but one's dressed as cowboys? For fuck's sake.

I shot at each one of them, aiming for their hearts. The bullets hit them, but they were severely unfazed. As in, if I didn't know any better, I'd say I hadn't even shot at them.

"So much for the gun," I sighed. I grimaced, raising my voice so they could hear me. "I don't know what she offered you, but she's a lying bitch!"

"One *billion* dollars for the head of Medusa," one of them said in a southern drawl.

I made a face.

"Yep. We've been hired to round you up and—"

"Sorry, but why are you talking like you just rolled out of a cowboy movie? We're in a modern city, not 1886."

"Well, we own a ranch called Cyclops Ranch and—"

"You're also dressed like some movie star," I interrupted.

"Yes, well, you see. We—"

"Most Cyclopes that I've seen are ugly, but the three of you aren't too bad. Except you could stand to lose the hats."

"Stop talking," one of them snarled. "You keep interrupting us."

"One billion dollars is an absurd amount of money. Who do you owe?"

"Can you pay it or not?" the middle one asked. "Otherwise, we ain't sparing you, lady danger noodle."

Lady danger noodle.

Had this fucking one eyed creep just called me lady *danger noodle?*

"You know what? Fuck all three of you." I shifted into my monster form and shot them the bird.

I took off towards the elevator doors, moving as quickly as possible.

I hit the up button and cursed under my breath as it took its sweet time to open. I turned around, ripping off my glasses as the three of them closed in on me.

One of them laughed. "The goddess gave us some protection for that. A little witchy spell."

Fuck me. Guns didn't work, neither did me turning them to stone.

"Well," I said. "I'm just gonna say this. If you kill me, my girlfriend will absolutely hunt you down and gut you."

"Doubt she'd be able to stop us," one of them snorted.

"I think you're underestimating her. She'll fry you into cyclops kebabs. She's the daughter of Zeus."

"Wait. You're telling me you're dating a *demigod?* But you're a monster."

I scoffed. "And? We're living in modern times, gentlemen. Get with the program. Also, whatever the goddess promised you, I guarantee you it will fall through. I used to work for her just like you are right now." *Why the fuck is the elevator taking so long?*

"Unless you can offer us a billion dollars, we're not letting you walk."

"That's a ridiculous amount of money," I argued. "You're fuckin' cowboys. Why do you need that much?"

"Why are we trying to reason with her? Just kill 'er and let's go, Wayne."

The elevator doors slid open. We all stared at each other for a moment, and then everything broke.

I hissed as I moved back into the elevator. I smashed the close button over and over as they attempted to cram in. I pulled a knife, stabbing at their hands until I got the doors shut.

I hit the floor button and dug into my bag, swiping my key card. The elevator jolted, the metal to the doors suddenly denting in.

Fuck.

I hit the floor button again, and luckily it began moving.

Three monsters down. Now I just had to face whatever creature was probably in my apartment.

CHAPTER 23

VENDETTA

M adeline

The elevator music was still going, grating on my nerves. I took the moment to load two more guns, holding one in each hand. My palms were sweating, which wasn't a good sign.

I had good instincts. Every single one of them was telling me this was a bad idea.

I wasn't putting my sunglasses back on. If anyone got in my way, they could simply turn to stone. Fuck them.

The elevator music was peaceful, it was annoying the fuck out of me. I pressed my lips together as the elevator rose, wondering what I would meet in my apartment.

Would it be another monster? Another enemy? Someone else working for the goddess?

My blood rushed in my ears as the elevator slowed to a stop. The light flickered as the doors slid open, creaking as they did.

"What the fuck?" I whispered.

I moved out of the elevator into the entry of my apartment. The entire space was filled with statues.

My statues.

The lights flickered on and off. The last of the golden rays of the sun were slowly disappearing. Every statue that I could see had a fading halo around them.

I wasn't alone here. I moved forward, holding up my guns, ready to kill whomever was here, slipping between two statues that blocked the main doorway.

The apartment was still completely wrecked. I had yet to come pick everything up, and at this point I wasn't sure I would. But between the piles of wreckage were the statues, and between the statues there was an eerie silence.

"I can sense you. I know that you're here, whoever you are," I whispered.

I slid between a statue of a woman and another of a man, wincing as my tail caught the base. It toppled over, crashing against the floor and shattering. Stone and plaster spread everywhere, broken bits flying.

I weaved through the living room, eyeing every statue. There were bloodstains on the floor still, dried, from Diego's body.

All the things that had happened.

The sadness that Percy had felt.

The worry, the pain.

All of it was because of a jealous goddess.

I withheld my rage. I had to proceed with a rational mind, or else things would fall apart.

One breath.

Two breaths.

Three.

I studied the statues. I half expected them to come back to life, especially the ones that used to be mortals.

Someone had brought all of my art here.

Every single piece.

The lights went out completely.

I came to the hallway and stared. The apartment was becoming darker and darker, every statue turning into shadows. I blinked as I moved past them, feeling a streak of regret that I was alone.

Percy would hate me when she woke up. She would have every right to. I would cause her pain and sadness.

I hated that.

I'm doing this for her. I'm doing this to save her.

I made it to the end of the hallway. Every light in the apartment had gone out except for the one behind this door. Light filtered out from beneath it. I reached for the doorknob and slowly turned it, pulling it open.

I didn't know what to expect behind the door, but my assistant certainly was not it.

"Ella," I whispered.

I stared in shock.

Ella.

Only Ella was not who I thought she was.

My assistant sat on the edge of my destroyed bed, her expression one I'd never seen on her face before. Hatred, amusement, disdain—all rolled up in her pert features.

My stomach dropped as everything continued to piece itself together. Ella had a key to my apartment. Ella would have been able to lure and kill Diego here. Ella would have known our addresses for the boxes. She was there the night the Minoan Bull attacked me.

She'd been here the whole time.

"You should be turning to stone," I said, keeping my voice emotionless. "If you were human, that is."

She grinned and shrugged. "Not human. And I've got to say,

I'm glad for it. You're not very nice to them, *Medusa*. And you have a serious addiction to caffeine."

This fucking bitch.

"I am a lot kinder to them than you are, *Discordia*." I swallowed hard, keeping my guns raised. "Why are you doing this? Why have you been playing the part of my assistant? Why did you take Clotho's hands? And why are you trying to destroy my life?"

"That's a lot of questions for someone who betrayed me," she chuckled. "You're a smart woman. Why do you *think*?"

"I never betrayed you," I said. "I simply stopped working for you. I explained everything to you. The Fates wanted me—"

"You *did* betray me. You left that demigod *alive*. And now, you're mated to her. You should have seen her face when I told her the two of you were mates. So much hope." Her smile was cruel. "She was so distraught when you were stabbed with the knife. I could see all her little thoughts going haywire as she realized she could have had a life with you. It was cruel of you to betray me for her, and then not even give her a chance."

"I've come here to negotiate with you. What do you want? What can I do to make you leave us alone?"

"There is nothing you can do. This is just a game to me," she said. "A means to an end. That's all you, your demigod, and your fate is to me."

Anger rolled through me. I glared at her, my grip tightening on my weapons.

"As for the Fates," she said. "They should not have interfered with me and my life. When they took you from me, they took one of my better weapons. Not my greatest, but a good one." Her voice was beyond condescending. "I don't like it when someone takes my toys. Doesn't make me want to play nice, does it?"

"I just want to live my life the same way that you do," I insisted.

"Then you should have killed that demigod when you had the chance."

A little growl left me. The snakes around my head hissed at her, more anger rolling through me.

She had asked me to kill my mate, knowing that Percy belonged to me. That she had asked me to do it was horrifying, looking back. She was a selfish bitch. Regardless of what happened, I was glad that I made the right decision.

I just regretted that Percy would suffer because there wasn't a way that I was going to win this fight with a goddess. But I would give it every single part of me that I could.

I pulled the trigger on both guns that I held. One went through her forehead, the other her chest. Blood burst from her, a gold vile liquid that spewed over me.

She merely laughed.

Strands of darkness crawled through the room. I moved forward, dodging an inky coil that reached for me. They were like hands pushing me further and further into the room.

I unloaded the rest of the bullets on her, at least feeling a hint of satisfaction as I put them all into her. It wasn't doing anything, but pulling the trigger was almost therapeutic.

Her body changed right before my eyes. I watched Ella become the goddess that I had known for centuries. The goddess that had used me over and over again to further herself.

"You know what?" I sneered. "You really are a shitty assistant."

Her form grew, her eyes turning black as she reached for me. I felt like I was trapped inside a tornado, the howling growing louder and louder.

There was no escaping this. It didn't matter how much I struggled, I couldn't break free of her grip. I snarled, snakes hissing and hissing. But none of it mattered. It didn't matter how strong I was.

I was a monster, and she was a goddess.

My heart pounded faster. I didn't want to die. I didn't want this to be the end, but I didn't see another way. She clearly hated me, and wanted me to suffer.

I shoved at her, letting out another growl. "If you're going to kill me just do it!" I shouted.

"I will not kill you," she said. "*Yet*. I have to have my fun first, you know this."

Horror washed over me as her face transformed. I watched as her hair became snakes, her skin taken on the same golden hue mine had. Wings burst from her back, spreading behind her.

She was becoming *me*.

"I wonder how your *mate* will feel when she dies at the hands of the woman she loves," she whispered.

She smiled, her face mirroring my own now. Every feature, wings to tail, scales and all.

"Leave her out of this," I said. I hated how much of a plea there was in my voice. "She has nothing to do with you or me or what happened—"

"She has *everything* to do with it. Everything."

The strands continued to bind me. She grabbed my face, forcing me to look into her eyes.

"I wonder how it feels for you to turn into stone," she whispered. "But don't worry, I won't let you die yet. I'll let you watch how everything unfolds. I will just turn you into a perfect statue so that you can't get in the way."

"No," I rasped. "No—you can't do this. You can't!"

She only smiled. I could already feel my muscles slowing, my heart rate dropping. My expression became immovable, every part of my body slowly freezing in place.

I was turning to stone.

But I wasn't dying.

Tears streamed down my cheeks until they, too, became stone. Everything stopped working, everything stopped moving.

Everything simply stopped.

CHAPTER 24

VILLAIN ERA

P ercy

"What the fuck?"

My words were groggy as my eyes slowly opened. I rolled over in bed, blinking until I could see straight. It was dark, and I was disoriented as hell.

My mouth was dry too. I scowled and lifted my head, looking around.

"Mads?" I called.

How long had I been asleep?

I looked over at the clock on the bedside table, and my eyes widened. There was no way it was almost midnight.

I sat up slowly, cursing under my breath. I felt like someone had drugged me.

I sat still for a moment, my heart slowly dropping.

"Mads?" I whispered. Tears blurred my vision as I got out of bed, stumbling. I caught myself screaming her name out. "Madeline?!"

I made my way to the door, leaning on the doorframe as I forced myself to breathe. I could feel something inside me slowly snapping, a hurt that was deeper than anything I'd ever felt before.

She drugged me.

I shoved the thought away. There was no way she would do that. She wouldn't hurt me like that.

The thought became a chant, my heart thundering as I made my way down the staircase. Slowly but surely, I was regaining all of my physical and mental awareness. The silence in the house was telling.

She wasn't dead.

That was the only reassurance I felt.

The bond between us had not weakened.

My mate was still alive.

But our home was empty.

"Madeline!" I screamed.

My shouts were met with silence.

Tears blurred my vision as I went to the kitchen, flipping on every light as I went.

A notepad sat on the corner of the counter, a pen next to it. I planted my hands to either side, my breaths becoming shakier and shakier.

Teardrops fell, blurring the ink. I read her note once, twice, three times, four...

I still couldn't comprehend the words.

I didn't believe it.

Why would she do this to me? Why would she abandon me like this?

I read her note again and shook my head. "Why? Why? Why?"

I searched the entire house, calling out her name over and over again as I looked for her. She had been in bed only a bit ago, but now she was gone.

She had left me.

I stepped out the front door, looking around wildly.

"You stupid fucking idiot," I whispered.

The words of her note were finally sinking in, although I couldn't understand why she had done this. She hadn't been kidnapped. She hadn't been forced to do something.

She'd simply gone.

But to who?

Who had she abandoned me for? Who was she fighting?

"Mistress. Are you looking for your car?" One of my guards was standing idly, his expression nervous.

My car was gone.

Not only had she fucking left me, she'd taken my fucking car too.

"If I find this bitch in one piece, I am going to chain her up in my basement," I seethed. "Where is my fucking car?"

"She took your car. She said she had to run an errand."

I marched over to him, the air crackling with electricity. He paled as I stopped in front of him.

"Where did she go?"

"She didn't say. She—"

"Find out," I said, my fingertips burning. "Find out by the time I come back downstairs or you will not live to see another day. And where the fuck is Eric?"

"I'll-I'll call him," he said. "I'll find out."

"You fucking better."

I left him and went back inside, storming upstairs. My mind seemed to float away, autopilot kicking in as I dressed for combat.

Maybe it was Orpheus. Maybe he'd done this. That's who she had mentioned in the note.

I picked out several blades. Several guns. I didn't need them, but I would use them with my demigod powers.

I could see my pain reflected in my closet mirror as I stared at myself, I hated it.

If something happened to her and I wasn't there to stop it, it would destroy me.

I ran back downstairs, meeting the guard's frightened gaze.

"She went to an apartment building in downtown Moirai. It's next to Andromeda."

"Awesome. Lucky for you."

I let out a low whistle. Within a few moments, Elektra came charging up the drive. I didn't even hesitate. I threw my leg over her, her wings already lifting into the sky as she felt my urgency.

"I don't care if mortals see us," I shouted over the wind. "We have to go as fast as we can. Take me to Orpheus first."

The sky rumbled with thunder, clouds gathering above us. I gripped her mane as she took us higher, faster.

Within a few minutes, we were in the city. She took me to a building downtown, one with an outdoor restaurant. I could see Orpheus sitting there, drinking wine as he ordered steak and scallops. Completely unaware that I was about to take him down.

Elektra swung down, her wings knocking over empty tables. People screamed and cried out as she landed on the rooftop patio.

I swung off, rushing towards Orpheus.

His eyes bulged as he stood, his mouth parting. "What the fuck are you doing?! There are humans—"

I raised my hand, feeling the storm in the air. Lightning answered me, streaking down from the sky. My body burned as

I directed it towards him, watching as it struck him, sending his body flailing.

The wind whipped around me as I marched towards him. People were running, screaming. I didn't care. I felt the first raindrops on my skin as I stood over him, breathing hard.

"Where is the knife?" I asked. "Give it to me now."

"You've lost your mind," he snarled. Sweat beaded on his brow, his eyes bulging. "Attacking me in front of mortals. You've lost it. Lost it!"

"I have," I whispered darkly. "Did you hear about my email, you fucking cunt? I know what you've done. I know that you betrayed me."

Fucking hell, I loved making this bastard squirm. He knew he'd done something wrong. He knew he'd fucked me over. And he knew I would slaughter him in a heartbeat if I decided to.

I held my lightning bolt and knelt down on his balls, applying my full weight. I pointed the electrical tip to his face, pinning him there until he cried out from the pain.

"Here's what's going to happen, Orpheus," I said. "You're going to give me the knife. You're going to tell me who hired you to give that knife to the Minoan Bull. Then you're going to get to live to see another fucking day because I am a *generous*, nice person."

"Fuck you," he rasped.

He brought my knee down harder and he cried out, tears filling his eyes.

"Speak or I'm going to castrate you with my fucking lightning bolt. *Where is the knife?*" I roared, thunder clapping again.

He let out a frustrated noise, but ultimately caved. "It's in my pocket," he said. "Take it. Take it, but bring it back. It belongs to me. It's mine. It's *mine*, Perseus."

I eased my knee back, but not the lightning bolt. I reached

down and pulled it out of his pocket, and then also held the blade to his neck.

I dragged the sharp tip over his skin. Blood welling, rolling down. His eyes widened, his head shaking. "I'll tell you. Stop this madness."

I wanted to stab him. I really did. Instead, I showed restraint. I showed mercy, which was more than anything he'd ever done for me.

"Who do you work for? Who asked you to do this?"

"A goddess," he croaked. "A goddess that I could not say no to. She made me do this, she made me betray you. I would never do that—"

I scoffed, releasing my bolt and standing back up. He remained on the ground, glaring at me. I pointed the knife at him. "You're a bastard." I kicked him as hard as I could between the legs. He howled in pain, curling into a fetal position. "Give me a fucking name."

"You bitch," he wheezed, groaning. "Eris. It's Eris. Discordia. Goddess of chaos. Medusa used to work for her and—"

I kicked him again. "Fuck you," I snarled. "If I make it out of this fight, best believe that I will be back on your fucking doorstep. If you ever double-cross me again, I will gut you and scatter your remains at your father's temple."

I took the knife and went back to Elektra. I gripped her mane and swung onto her back. She snorted, black smoke curling from her nostrils as rain fell.

Orpheus was still groaning on the ground. I took one last look, fuming.

"Go," I told Elektra.

She sped up into the sky.

Madeline's apartment wasn't far from here. It wouldn't take us long to get there. I wrapped my arms around her neck, holding onto her as I whispered what I needed her to do.

Thunder cracked above us. The rain poured harder as we flew through the sky. It pelted me, the storm a mirror to everything I felt. The agony, the fear, the pain, the rage. Her black wings spread to either side, the feathers glistening.

I gripped the knife in one hand, readying myself as we came to the building. She flew towards the top, the glass window reflecting the flashes of lightning.

You better be alive, Mads, or I'm going to end the whole fucking world.

CHAPTER 25

CHAOS

P ercy

Shards burst everywhere as I flew through the glass window. Elektra landed hard, the two of us knocking into several statues. I was already sliding off her back, ignoring my disorientation.

I shook glass and stone off my body, Elektra doing the same. I steadied myself, looking around.

This wasn't how we had left the apartment.

I drew my lightning bolt, casting a fluorescent blue glow over everything in the room. I held it in one hand, the knife in the other. Madeline's art had almost completely taken over the place, her belongings smashed.

Statues of people frozen in time littered the entire space, creating a daunting maze. They covered every corner, crammed together with no rhyme or reason.

I shook my head, bewildered. Whoever had done this was fucking with my mate.

That pissed me off.

This was the type of mental game that twisted someone up. That, coupled with the eerie silence, made my stomach clench.

Elektra snorted nervously, pawing the ground with her hoof.

"Wait on the roof," I told her softly.

She snorted in protest, but ultimately listened. She flew back out the window, more glass shattering over the floor.

I watched her go, her dark figure disappearing.

I lifted the bolt, the air crackling around me. I could feel the charge, fueled by my rage and worry.

It was difficult to keep a clear head. Madeline leaving had hurt more than anything else, and I was nursing the ache while also desperately wanting to know if she was okay.

Something was wrong. Very wrong.

It had been a long time since I'd been in this state. I was gearing up for a battle. No, not a battle. I was about to go to war with my enemy. I was about to slay a goddess.

Because of course Madeline's enemy would be a goddess. And her enemy was mine.

There was a first time for everything. I couldn't say that I was happy this was how it was, but I would get my answers once I rescued my mate.

My stomach was still uneasy, but I remained focused. I took a step forward, wincing as my boot crunched over the broken glass. I tiptoed around most of it, weaving between several statues. I listened intently, doing my best to notice anything out of place.

I stepped around a couple of statues and then paused, looking up to my left. My eyes widened as I met the face of one of the Fates.

Clotho.

I scowled. I didn't remember Madeline ever sculpting her. I

felt a shiver work through me as I studied her. She looked exactly like her, except she was missing her hands.

I took one last glance at her and then continued on. My instincts drove me down the hallway, going towards the only light that seemed to be on in the entire apartment.

"Percy..."

"Mads?" I asked, my heart jumping.

I took off running, kicking open the bedroom door. The wood splintered as it flew open, revealing everything behind it.

Madeline was at the center of the room on the floor, blood dripping from her. There was a knife in her stomach, her monstrous form curled in on itself. Around her, there were several statues and more destroyed furniture.

My gaze flickered to the statue that looked exactly like her. I shook my head and then rushed forward, kneeling next to her.

"What happened?" I growled. I couldn't feel her pain.

She let out a sharp cry. I cursed under my breath, pulling her torso into my lap. The snakes around her head didn't hiss like they normally did. Her wings split to the side, and I reached around, grabbing the hilt of the blade.

"Fuck. Let me pull this knife out. It's going to be okay, love, I promise."

"Do what you must," she said dramatically.

I frowned and yanked the knife out, tossing it to the side.

"Madeline, what the fuck is going on?" I asked. "You drugged me. You left me." I couldn't keep the pain from my voice, even holding her while she healed.

She tilted her head back, looking up at me. Her diamond pupils reflected malice, something I'd never seen on her face towards me before. Not even when we'd first met. "Maybe I just didn't want to be with you anymore."

Part of me broke. Her words snapped me in half. My lips parted, but words could not come out.

"I appreciate you rescuing me though," she said casually.

"What do you mean?" I scoffed. "Of course I would come to rescue you. We are mates. You are *mine*."

She slowly sat up, pulling herself away from me. I attempted to tug her back, but then she yanked herself from my grip.

"I just don't want this anymore, she said. You aren't worth it to me. You're a demigod, and I am a monster. The two of us aren't meant to be together."

"You don't mean that," I whispered. My body was shaking, tears blurring my vision. "You don't mean that. I know you love me. You've loved me as long as I have loved you."

"I was just using you," she said. "Using you to get what I wanted. Maybe that's what it was."

"Using me for what?" I yelled. "What would you possibly use me for?"

"Power, sex, money. The usual. What else?"

I let out a growl and reached for her. She moved out of the way, her expression growing angrier.

"I don't want you," she snarled. "I don't want you, and I never will. You're not good enough for me. You never will be."

"You're lying," I growled. "You're lying, and I don't know why. Why are you lying to me right now?"

"I'm not lying," she snapped. "Why would I lie to you? You know that I'm telling you the truth."

I shook my head, completely confused. I watched her move around the room, her gaze tracking over the statues. She was so casual as she moved, as if I hadn't just found her curled up on the floor with a knife inside of her stomach. As if we hadn't gone through so much together in the last couple of weeks.

This wasn't the woman that I loved. This wasn't the woman that I knew.

My blood rushed to my ears, my gaze rolling over to the other statue.

The one of Madeline, that looked exactly like her.

I would have felt her stab. I would have felt the knife wound as I pulled it out through our bond.

I hadn't felt that at all.

She wasn't lying.

I took a step back, drawing Orpheus' knife. I gripped the handle, slowly drawing my lightning bolt too.

"You're right," I said.

She froze where she stood, her back stiffening. She let out a slow, feminine laugh. One that sent a chill through my blood.

"I've got to hand it to you," she chuckled. "It didn't take you too long to figure it out. Although I expected *better* from the daughter of Zeus."

"What did you do with my mate?" I snarled. "Where is she? *Where is she?!*"

"Where do you think?" she laughed, gesturing to the statue that looked like Madeline.

Fuck.

"Mads," I whispered.

She was unmoving, truly a statue. I shook my head, rage rolling through me. That's why I couldn't feel her here. She was frozen, and it felt as if there were a wall between us.

"You turned my mate into a statue."

"Wouldn't you say she deserved it?" Her form shifted from Madeline's to someone that was much less familiar. She was a goddess that I didn't remember crossing paths with.

Which meant the others hated her.

It made sense. I already hated her.

"Turn her back. Release her," I gritted out.

"Who are you to make demands, little demigod?"

"Release. My. Mate."

"I think not," she said. "I think I'm going to make her watch me kill you. And then I'll keep her alive and frozen for a couple thousand years so that Hades may not reunite you. How brilliant is that?"

My muscles moved for me. I let out a growl as I rushed towards her, her fury apparent in her expression. She moved out of the way, the lights in the room bursting. Darkness followed, the lights of the city and my lightning the only thing illuminating us.

She pulled a knife from thin air, one that had an inky black blade. I dodged right as she thrust it towards me.

I jabbed at her with my bolt, catching her arm. She hissed, the smell of burnt flesh surrounding us.

She hit me hard enough that I fell back, pain rattling my skull.

I hit the floor hard, my grip loosening on the knife. It slid out of my hand. I rolled to the side as she lunged for me. She grabbed my hair, pulling me back.

"You're being such a hero," she snarled.

The two of us rolled, her strength matching mine.

I drew on my powers, electricity bursting from me with enough power that she flew back. She knocked one statue, smashing it into a million pieces.

Her eyes burned with hate as she slowly got up. "Careful," she whispered. "Would hate for that to happen to your *mate*."

There was a quiet moment, brief and still. It was the blink of an eye, and the both of us were moving again.

I snatched up the knife again and tackled her to the floor, yelping as she rolled me over shards of stone. I felt them crunch against my body, ignoring the pain that followed as we wrestled.

I punched her as hard as I could, getting a moment of satisfaction from the sound of bones breaking. She screeched, raking her fingernails over my cheek.

My knee came up, wedging between her chest and mine. I used the momentum to throw her off, attempting to keep my grip on the knife.

The knife that would supposedly kill anything.

She laughed as she got up again, her expression becoming crazed. Blood dripped from a busted lip, her eyes burning.

"I've been taking it easy on you," she said. "You think you're strong enough to get me with that blade? Try saving *her* first."

I was already moving towards Madeline as she said that. She lifted her hand, sending a blast of dark magic careening towards Madeline.

"No!" I shouted.

I threw myself in front of her right before it struck, gasping as it impaled me like a thousand blades.

Pain. So much pain. I looked down as my knees hit the floor, gold blood leaking out.

"Fuck," I wheezed.

She laughed as she walked over to me. I looked up at her as she smiled. She took a fistful of my hair and dragged me forward, tossing me onto my back like a rag doll.

Tears rolled down my cheeks as the pain came again in mind numbing waves. This wasn't the sort of injury I was sure I could live through.

She was a goddess.

My gaze went past her to Madeline. Frozen in time.

I started to cry harder.

I didn't want my last images of her to be stuck like that.

"Madeline," I rasped.

Discordia stepped over me, leaning down with a wicked grin. "She can hear you," she whispered. "She can see you. She can see me. I bet she hates herself so much right now."

My grip on the blade tightened. I pushed all of my energy towards it, willing myself through the blaring pain to make this count.

"*Fuxkyoo,*" I mumbled.

"What was that?" she asked, leaning in closer.

I brought the blade up in one swift motion, burying the knife straight into her heart. Her eyes widened, a gasp leaving her.

"I said *fuck you.*"

CHAPTER 26

HANDS OF FATE

M adeline

The moment the knife pierced her heart, my body was able to move again. I gasped, crying as I fell forward.

Discordia howled, but her body was already beginning to turn to ash. I looked up, watching as the goddess simply crumbled, the blade clanking against the ground.

Gold blood pooled around Percy. She let out a soft groan and slumped completely against the floor, wheezing.

"Percy," I rasped. "Percy."

I crawled to her, dragging my tail behind me. Her blood wet my palms as I reached for her, pulling her into my arms. Her silver hair was covered with it, her eyes fluttering.

"Percy," I said again. I couldn't stop saying her name. I hated that this is how everything had happened.

This was all my fault. I should've known that the goddess would have been prepared for me. I should have told Percy everything when I started putting the pieces together, but instead of relying on my mate, I had done what I always did in the past. I had done everything alone, which was a weakness, not a strength.

"You stupid, stupid woman," she whispered, her voice a croak.

"I'm so sorry," I cried. "I'm so, so sorry. I should've told you everything, but I didn't want to risk you getting hurt."

She let on a soft hum, forcing her eyes open. "Don't you know I would do anything for you?" she asked. "That I would fight anyone for you. It hurt more that you left me."

"I know," I sobbed. I swept her hair back from her face, holding her tight. I ran my hands down her body, feeling her wounds. They weren't healing.

They should have been healing.

She was a demigod.

"You should be healing right now."

"She was a goddess," Percy sighed, her eyes slowly closing again. "I don't know if I'm coming back from this, my love."

"You will," I said. "You will. You have to. I'm so sorry."

My entire body was trembling. I held onto her as her eyes fluttered, her breaths becoming rattled. I could feel her pain, her sadness, her love. All of it shared between us, sifting through me like grains of sand through fingers.

"Did you sculpt Clotho?" Percy rasped.

"What? Why does that matter?" I asked.

The light faded from her eyes.

"No, no, no," I sobbed. "No. This can't happen."

I looked around wildly, seeing the statues that were still in the room. Taking it all in. Everything was ruined, completely utterly wrecked.

Discordia had tried to take everything for me. She'd wrecked my belongings, destroying countless pieces of art.

None of that mattered.

I would take her destroying every single possession I owned as long as I could keep Percy.

I could feel her heart slowing, every beat becoming lethargic. I let out a sob, my thoughts racing.

"No," I cried. "It was supposed to be me. Not you. It was never supposed to be you."

I could feel her going. I held her tighter, sobs wracking my entire body as she slipped further and further from me.

"Madeline."

A muffled voice called from outside my room. I looked up, staring through the doorway. The lights had come back on, but all I could see were statues.

I looked back down at Percy, my vision blurring with tears.

I'd never sculpted Clotho.

I released her and rose quickly.

"Madeline!"

My body moved in a blur. I rushed out of the room, going down the hall. I turned to the right, a curse leaving me.

"Clotho? What are you doing?" I said.

She had collapsed on the floor, blood pooling around her. Her body trembled, her eyes burning with anger.

"Where are my hands?" she asked, holding up her mutilated wrists. "Please."

"Will you save Percy?" I asked.

Her expression flashed. "Get my hands. Now."

"Will you save her if I do?"

"I'll do more than save her, Madeline. Get me my fucking hands."

I felt Percy go.

The mated bond went silent.

Everything stopped.

The agony was so overwhelming, I nearly crumpled. I

looked up to meet Clotho's pleading gaze. A pained shout left
me but I turned, rushing through the wreckage to the black bag
in the foyer. I dug through it, pulling out her hands and taking
them back to her. I unwrapped them, starting with her right
hand first. I held it to her wrist.

"Close your eyes."

I did as she commanded. Light flooded the room, so bright I
could see it even with my eyes closed, followed by blazing heat.
My heart thundered in my chest.

"Now, the other."

We did the same with her left hand. I closed my eyes again,
more light flashing.

"Open your eyes."

I did. She looked down at her hands, faint scars around her
wrists. She glowered.

"How could you let this happen?" I whispered.

Her head shot up. "This was not my doing."

"But you're stronger than them," I said. "You and your
sisters are stronger than the gods. How could she trick you?"

"I underestimated her," Clotho growled, shaking her head. I
was shocked she was even honest about that. She let out a sigh
and then moved her fingers, golden threads appearing. "Go to
your mate, Madeline. Her heart will beat again. I will not be
here when you return, but will speak to you at a later time. Go
be with her, Madeline. That cunt messed a lot of things up, but
she was correct about the two of you being meant for each
other."

I left her immediately, rushing back to Percy's side. Right as
I pulled her against me, I felt the soft flutter.

Fuck.

I sobbed again, holding her tighter than ever as she drew in a
sharp breath, followed by a groan.

"You're going to wear my collar," she rasped.

A blubbering laugh left me. She reached up, grabbing my face and planting a heavy kiss. I melted against her, still crying as I kissed her the way I should have centuries ago.

She pressed her forehead to mine. "I love you. You will never leave me like that again."

"I swear I never will," I whispered. "I'm so sorry. I love you so much. Every moment I was frozen I felt like I was dying watching you fight her. I felt like I was dying over and over. And then I felt you go. I felt you leave me. And I know that's how I made you feel and I'm so sorry."

"Baby," she murmured, stealing a tender kiss. "I forgive you. We made it. We survived."

She leaned back, wiping away my tears.

"We'll never have to fight alone again," she said. "Those days are behind us."

I nodded, my throat closing up. "I don't know how you love me."

"How can I not? You're everything to me," she said. "I love every part of you, Madeline, even the broken parts. I'm yours."

I hiccuped, holding back more tears. I finally exhaled, feeling all the tension exit with it.

"Was that really Clotho?" she asked.

"Yes. I should tell you everything."

"Yes, you should."

So I did. The two of us stayed entwined as I explained Ella, the boxes, the train ride years ago where I was supposed to kill her. I told her about Discordia and how I'd made it as a monster all these years. The things I'd done, the things I regretted.

I told her everything.

I told her things I'd never said aloud.

She didn't judge me for a single thing. She didn't hate me for any of it. She just listened, occasionally stealing another kiss.

I blew out a breath as I finished, feeling free for the first time since I'd been a monster.

Truly free.

Percy finally smirked. "I knew you had a thing for me on the train. You wanted me in this bloody mafia so bad."

"Shut up. You had no idea."

"I absolutely had a feeling."

The two of us grinned like idiots.

"Fuck," I sighed. "I have it bad. Real bad."

"Yeah, we both do. Wouldn't change anything about it."

I nodded, leaning against her. A silence settled between us, a comfortable one. It was like putting on your favorite scarf or curling up with a favorite tattered book.

"I have an idea," she finally said, giving me a soft smile.

"What?" I asked.

"I say we take a shower. Get cleaned up. Change into some very expensive clothing that makes us look hot. And finally go to our breakfast date and get some mimosas. Not the virgin kind."

"Oh. I thought you wanted me to quit drinking."

"I think we can make an exception."

She took my hands, the two of us rising. Normally, I might have changed back into my mortal form, but for once...

I didn't feel the need to.

"I wonder if your shower is still working," she hummed.

"We can find out. And I'm sure there are some articles of clothing not ruined...although..."

I trailed off as I looked around us, raising my brows.

All the statues were gone. My bed was made, and there was no sign that any destruction had ever occurred. I turned around, peering down the hallway. The door was unbroken, all the art pristine. The two of us went out to the living room, where everything had been restored to normal.

"That was kind of her," Percy said.

The sun was rising over Moirai now. It hadn't felt like so many hours had passed, but dealing with a goddess could warp time. The clouds were turning pink, the storm having passed. Percy slid her hand into mine, the two of us standing in peace.

"Let's get ready for our date," I said, squeezing her hand.

"And after that, I have some shopping to do."

"You're really going to make me wear that, huh?"

"Don't worry. We can have a day collar and a night collar. You'll like them both."

"Your taste is questionable, darling. Perhaps I should pick them out."

She laughed, tugging me back down the hall to my shower. "You will wear whatever I pick out for you, kitten. Including what I ask you not to wear."

I snorted. "What shouldn't I wear?"

"Well, first, I'm thinking you can skip the underwear for breakfast."

A shiver of anticipation worked through me as she pulled me into the bathroom, pushing me against the wall.

"Are you sure we'll make it to breakfast on time?" I whispered.

"Let's call it a brunch."

Her lips met mine, and I melted against her.

I breathed her in, loving her with every part of my soul. Thankful that while it had taken us so long to finally come together, that we'd made it.

Not every monster had to have a tragic ending. She had taught me that.

She'd taught me I didn't have to hide anymore.

That I could be *me* and still be loved.

Demigod and monster.

Hero and villain.

Two women with hearts of stone that had lived centuries alone.

We didn't have to be alone anymore.

She paused our kiss, letting out a soft moan. "I love you. Forever and always."

"I love you too."

All I could think was that I was thankful that she'd washed up on my shore all those years ago.

Perhaps it had been fate after all.

A Hero's Ending

Six Months Later

P ercy

The waves crashed against the shore, the sky clear blue and not a cloud in sight. I looked up the beach to where Madeline laid out in the sun in her full monster form, her scales glittering like jewels. Gray cliffs rose in the distance, marking the end of our tiny getaway island.

We'd taken a two-month trip around Europe, stopping in Greece to destroy the rest of Poseidon's temple for fun. That had been on the news, all the headlines claiming that the old gods were angry. I doubted they even cared.

We'd gone to Paris, London, Rome. I'd successfully shrugged off all our mafia responsibilities to the Minoan Bull, of all creatures, while we were on vacation. He was a good leader, despite our rocky beginning.

Orpheus was still alive. I'd also, despite truly not wanting to, given him his knife back. None of the other leaders trusted him now, and his business was suffering for it.

The island we were on was vacant. I'd enjoyed every moment of peace we'd been able to grab. The island we'd met on so long ago was now consumed by the sea, but it had been almost poetic to end up back up on one with her in the same part of the world.

It was perfect. I could hunt and chase her to my heart's desire.

I continued my walk up the beach, slowing as I neared her.

"You're going to burn," I teased.

She opened one eye, squinting at me. "I'm getting my vitamins."

I snorted and lowered myself, straddling her hips.

"Hey," she giggled.

"Hey," I said.

I leaned down to kiss her, but something hit me in the head. I cursed, rolling to the side.

"What the fuck?" she growled.

We both watched as a black bird circled above us and then vanished.

As in—we blinked, and it was gone.

I looked to my side, seeing an envelope.

We both stared at it.

"We can ignore it," she said, pressing her lips together.

I winced. We could. But ignoring a letter from the Fates was never a good idea.

I picked it up and flipped it over, seeing the Three Fates seal.

I broke it and pulled out the piece of paper, reading the words scrawled there.

DEAR PERCY AND MADELINE,

BOTH OF YOU HAVE SERVED US WELL. YOU HAVE PLAYED YOUR ROLES THROUGHOUT HISTORY AND HAVE WALKED THE PATH YOU WERE DESTINED TO WALK.

IF YOU WISH TO RETIRE FROM THE THREE FATES MAFIA, YOU CAN DO SO WHILE STILL KEEPING THE BENEFITS PREVIOUSLY GIVEN. THE MINOAN BULL SERVES US WELL AND CAN TAKE YOUR PLACE. THE CHOICE IS YOURS.

CLOTHO, LACHESIS, AND ATROPOS

I read it once more, blowing out a breath.

"Well? Are we being drafted back home?"

"No," I said, looking up at her.

She scowled. I handed her the letter, waiting for her to read it. She did the same, reading through it several times before she put the paper down, laying back.

I laid down next to her, the two of us staring up at the cloudless sky.

"There's more to life than power," I whispered.

"I know."

"We've worked for someone else our entire lives. The gods. The Fates."

"I know."

"We'd be able to do whatever we wanted."

"I know." Her voice carried a little more excitement this time.

Did I want to give up my position? Did I want to walk away from that life? I'd gotten used to being a brutal bitch the last few decades. And even before that, I'd constantly been involved in the mortal world somehow. Their wars, their tragedies...

We would be able to just live.

And be happy.

"I would like to leave the mafia," she whispered. "I would like to lay on the beach with you. To sculpt art with my hands. To laugh and fuck and exist without someone else holding my life over my head."

"Me too," I said.

We both looked at each other.

"So is that it then?" she whispered. "Is that what you want to do? What *I* want to do? We've done so much for them. For everyone."

I slowly nodded, our hands sliding together. "I think so. I like the sound of Percy, demigod, wife to Madeline, and retired hero."

"Madeline, sexy monster, wife to Percy, and retired villain."

"They ran off to be gay and merry together. After killing the goddess of chaos and saving one of the Fates, they were never seen again. But if you look up at the stars, you might notice to *monsterpussyexplorer* constellation which was named after their passionate love—"

She cackled, her cheeks turning bright pink. I wasn't sure if it was my words or the sun. The locket collar I'd given her sat against her collarbone, the engraved phrase "*She is my god and I bow to her*" gleaming.

"Why did they turn everyone into fucking stars?"

I laughed with her until the two of us could barely breathe. Finally, I sighed.

"We deserve a happy ending, Mads."

"I think we got one," she said. "I think this is it."

"No one ever got this in the history books," I murmured.

"All of those history cunts were drunk," she snorted. "I bet they told the stories wrong. Remember? Everyone thinks you're a man."

"And everyone thinks I cut off your head."

We both burst into a fit of giggles now, a weight being lifted from us that had been holding us down since our beginnings. I pulled her towards me, the two of us rolling until she ended up on top of me, her wings blocking out the glare of the sun.

She raised a brow, her fangs glistening because neither one of us could stop smiling.

"How should we celebrate?" she asked.

"Hmmm. How about I fuck you until the sun goes down?"

She smirked. "And then?"

"And then I'll fuck you until the sun comes up."

"Deal."

Woman, monster, villain—I would forever be hers, and she would forever be mine.

ALSO BY CLIO EVANS

CREATURE CAFE SERIES

Little Slice of Hell

Little Sip of Sin

Little Lick of Lust

Little Shock of Hate

Little Piece of Sass

Little Song of Pain

Little Taste of Need

Little Risk of Fall

Little Wings of Fate

Little Souls of Fire

Little Kiss of Snow: A Creature Cafe Christmas Anthology

WARTS & CLAWS INC. SERIES

Not So Kind Regards

Not So Best Wishes

Not So Thanks in Advance

Not So Yours Truly

Not So Much Appreciated

FREAKS OF NATURE DUET

Doves & Demons

Demons & Doves

CLIO'S CREATURES

Hello Creatures!

My name is Clio Evans and I am so excited to introduce myself to you! I'm a lover of all things that go bump in the night, fancy peens, coffee, and chocolate.

IF you had the chance to be matched with a monster- what kind would you choose?!

Let me know by joining me on FB and Instagram. I'm a sucker for werewolves (and plague doctors ;)) to this day.

THANK YOU

Sarah, Sarah, and Kim— y'all are the GOAT. Thank you so much for your help and support.

Made in the USA
Monee, IL
12 April 2024

56447204R00154